IVANA GEČEK
BYE-BYE, BABAROGA

Ivana Geček
BYE-BYE, BABAROGA

ISBN
ebook 978-953-8360-31-2
paperback 978-953-8360-32-9

EDITED BY
Vesna Kurilić

COVER BY
Antonio Filipović

Rijeka, 2024

shtriga.com
shtrigabooks@gmail.com

Ivana Geček

Bye-Bye, Babaroga

Rijeka, 2024

To all the people who have yet to find the courage to tell their story (or find what it is).
Don't worry—you'll get there.

CONTENTS

PART I:
THE SURGEON

Chapter 1

KAJA'S NERVES ARE GETTING thinner. Each kilometer feels like a grater inside her head, slowly scraping her brain cells away—by the time they finally arrive at the lodge, she imagines her brain would have turned into a pink sludge, and she'd hop out of the car like a dumb, drooling zombie.

Tihana, on the other hand, has different concerns. "I hope the weather gets better once we're there. It's been freaking *pouring* since we sat in the car," she whines, rustling through her bag. "Ugh, I bet it's going to be cold up in the hills, right? I should've packed warmer clothes, but it's still October, and a heavier jacket is more for November, don't you think? What did you bring, a parka? Very sensible, kudos to you. But well, it's only three days, so I guess I'll survive. Dammit, where the hell are my snacks? I swear I brought them with me..."

Kaja sighs, gripping the steering wheel. Three days, indeed. She's starting to regret offering Tihana the ride; it's been about two hours since they left Zagreb, and she's been blabbing away like a wind-up toy. Kaja imagines that's what having a younger sister feels like. Exhausting.

"We're going to be so late," Tihana laments from the passenger seat, opening a bag of chips. The sound of chewing fills up the car, merging with the thump of rain against the windshield. "Take some," she munches, nudging at Kaja with the bag.

Outside, the wind howls, making the third tractor they've been stuck behind for the last half an hour slow down even more. A humorless huff escapes Kaja's throat—how could she have forgotten the joys of taking country roads in Zagorje?

"Oh, c'mon," Kaja mutters, squinting at the blurry, tractor like shape. "Fucking move." Her hand itches to smack the horn. A sudden bump in the road makes the car sway, eliciting a grunt from Kaja and a squeak from Tihana. Kaja's too tired for this. Irritated, she moves to honk the frustration out of her system—out of all the places, why did Sandra have to pick out Kalnik as their team building headquarters?

"Don't honk," Tihana whimpers around a mouthful of chips. "The last thing we need is for some local hicks to attack us with pitchforks."

Kaja snorts. Coming from Zagorje, she knows that the *Wrong Turn* scenario Tihana is probably imagining is not really likely to happen, though being chased by some feral people still sounds endlessly better than the forced, corporate hell of a team building they're heading to. Not even the medical profession is safe from its grasp, apparently.

She smacks the horn once, just to get Tihana riled up.

When the tractor finally takes a turn off the main road, Kaja steps on the gas, carefully threading the roads bending in front of them. The rain mellows out to a soft drizzle, clearing the view. Fields spread beside them, gray and washed-out in the gloomy weather. Tihana pulls down her window, pointing excitedly at a herd of cows.

"Cows!" she exclaims with childlike glee. *Cows*, Kaja internally agrees. However, as the stink of manure starts filling up the car, Tihana pulls the window up quickly, gagging dramatically.

After a while, Kalnik finally comes into view, peeking through a cloud of fog gathered around the foot of the hills. Kaja sighs in relief. Her wayward GPS brought them to the right place after all. Tihana's been chattering away in the background, consistent and soothing like a white noise machine.

"Kaja, are you listening?"

"Yes," Kaja lies, making Tihana groan in frustration.

"No, you're not!" she accuses. "I asked, who would you rather do: that guy who came to fix our water cooler, or the guy who came to fix our air conditioner?"

Kaja frowns—she'd vaguely noticed the guys coming into the clinic in the first place, let alone recalled their faces.

"I don't remember what they looked like," she answers diplomatically.

"Bullshit. How could you not remember? They were so *hot*."

Kaja shrugs. She can see Tihana's pout out of the corner of her eye.

"C'mon, you have to pick one," she urged. "You must have some kind of a preference. I mean, the water cooler guy was just like, *woof*."

Kaja rolls her eyes, hoping Tihana drops the subject. This is starting to feel like a high school sleepover, and being back near her hometown is exhausting enough. She turns on the radio, letting the noise of a hackneyed local station thwart Tihana's probing.

"All right then, keep your secrets," Tihana yells across the music, "but you're no fun!" She starts to sing along with the radio, and Kaja's more than happy to tune her out again, glancing at the hills spreading in front of them.

Kaja yawns, running on a few hours of sleep yet again. Her eyes itch like sandpaper.

Three days, she thinks, blinking at the bumpy road. *Three days, indeed.*

***

A few months ago, Kaja got called into Robert's office. At that point, she'd been working in the clinic for almost a year. It was a nice change of pace from working in the ER, where she did her internship.

"This isn't the right place for you," her superior had said at the end of her term, shaking her head at Kaja's dark circles and woozy decision-making. "Try getting a job in some private clinic." That's how she ended up in Beautifully Beautiful, a clinic specializing in cosmetic treatments and surgery. After a year of impossible shifts, overbearing responsibilities, and one too many close calls, she's gladly welcomed the world of filler injections and facial tucks. Most days, she operated on autopilot—jab, inject, tighten, tuck, repeat. Easy as that. The repetition and triviality of the procedures soothed her mind like a balm.

The clinic consists of only a few doctors and a couple of nurses. Robert, the boss, is the head surgeon. Like a typical boss, he doesn't do much of anything. Most days he parades aimlessly around the clinic to "keep the situation under control", as he likes to put it. He often disappears for hours on end—usually behind a locked door—with his HR consultant Sandra, leaving the surgeries and procedures to the other surgeon, nicknamed "Butcher".

Butcher is Robert's old college buddy, specializing in liposuction. With his gruff articulation and giant, intimidating build, it's a wonder he hasn't scared off the little regular patients they have left. In between surgeries, he can be found in their small lounge area, draining down some beer, along with their dentist Dejan. They complement each other well: Dejan's natural gift for mindless shit-talking shines against Butcher's monosyllabic nature.

If Dejan isn't sharing his unwarranted opinions on the whichever hot topics are presently burning on the Internet, he's probably shoving a phone up someone's face, showcasing the gallery of buck teeth veneers he's made in the last few years, or bragging about his dad, who's a passionate member of the right-winged political party that's currently soiling their country.

Kaja never enters the common area willingly, avoiding it like the plague.

The only colleague she can put up with is Tihana, their esthetician. Even though her sunny disposition and bubbly personality sometimes gets on her nerves, Kaja never turns down her company on their lunch break, occasionally—and secretly—enjoying her blabbering and food-sharing.

"Good luck!" Tihana chirped as Kaja passed her by on the way to Robert's office.

"You're probably wondering why I called you in today," he said as Kaja came in, clasping his hands in front of him and pinning her down with an unreadable look. That was, actually, true—Kaja could never read her boss properly, as the layers of botox stored under his skin had cemented his face into an expression of polite constipation most of the time.

She nodded, sitting down on a smooth, leather chair.

Robert contorted his face into something resembling a smile, eyes crinkling the best they could.

He turned to his side, where Sandra was lounging back into her seat, nyloned legs crossed. Her strong perfume scorched Kaja's nose.

"Don't worry, darling, it's nothing bad," Sandra quipped as her red lips stretched into a patronizing smirk. There was a new, shiny necklace around her neck. Kaja stifled a sigh. At the rate new jewelry keeps adorning Sandra's body, it's a miracle they haven't gone bankrupt yet.

Uncomfortable silence stretched among the three of them. Kaja shifted in her seat, stealing glances around the office. It was actually really nice in here. The chair was divinely comfortable under her butt. Robert's medical certificates hung on the freshly painted walls, next to abstract paintings Kaja was sure Robert didn't have the capacity to appreciate. A small, stylized sculpture of a woman's body lay neatly on the shelf, holding a bunch of health magazines and medical books in place.

'Times are hard,' Robert had said a few months ago, but looking at the state of his office, or the giant, fancy wristwatch adorning his wrist, the times were definitely not that hard for everyone. Ever since they'd downsized a while ago, moving from their posh office in the city center to this industrial zone at the edge of town, the procedure room Kaja had been given wasn't really a welcoming space.

'It's an up-and-coming neighborhood,' was all Robert offered as they hauled their equipment into the building. 'We'll get this place spruced up in no time.' Judging by the peeling paint and old, shabby surgical chairs in Kaja's office, he wasn't in a hurry. At least it smelled good, due to the fresh laundry-scented air freshener Tihana gifted her.

The anticipation was getting the better of Kaja.

"So, uh, how are you—" she began, but Robert interrupted her, lifting a well manicured hand in the air.

"Let's skip the small talk, shall we? I'd prefer to get right to the chase." He cleared his throat, leaning toward Kaja. "As you may have noticed, business has been slow lately," he started. "Customers haven't been coming in as usual."

Beside him, Sandra nodded gravely, running a hand through her long, ironed hair. "You see, dear, the pandemic really took a toll on us," she said. "People have shifted their priorities. Cosmetic surgery fell back. For some, apparently, being *beautifully beautiful* isn't a matter of import." She snickered, amused, but quickly pulled herself back together once Robert glared her down with his constipated stare. "As you know, we have tried to keep the customers interested with various deals and discounts," she continued, shifting in her seat as much as her tight, pencil shirt allowed her, "but it didn't really attract the kind of buzz we were hoping for."

Kaja nodded, keeping her face carefully neutral and polite. Even if she wanted to, she could never forget the *Drain it: 2 for 1 Liposuction Discount* or *Like Mother, Like Daughter: A Nose Job Package for Two*.

"Sandra assured me that you'd be better suited to the task," Robert cut in. "After all, you're the newest hire. A fresh set of eyes might do us some good."

Kaja blinked. "Uh," she said, "which task are we talking about?"

Robert looked at her like she'd grown a second head. After a few moments, he barked out a laugh. Sandra joined him, sneering like a hyena.

"Why, to make us money, of course!" he clarified. "To fix this dry spell we've been in!" He leans back into his seat, a resolved look on his face. "Butcher and I are old, and Dejan's only interested in teeth. Tihana's a nice girl, but she only knows how to squeeze pimples. But you, you're different from the rest of us. There's an aura of misery hanging around you. Perhaps you would guess what the common people want more accurately, than say, me or Butcher."

And well, Kaja couldn't really argue with that. She certainly is miserable enough. With her lonely existence, deprecating self-image, and fragile dignity, she is definitely close to the susceptible mindset of their average customer; it's a wonder, actually, that she hasn't stuck some filler up her own face yet, the way she always longed just to fit in.

Coming up with a snappy marketing campaign was way out of her depth, though. Before she could gauge how to respond, Sandra chimed in.

"You've got a lot of potential in you. It would be a shame not to explore it," she said, nodding her head in agreement. "Of course, we'll be with you every step of the way. I'll share with you my tools of the trade. Visualization, manifestation, you name it. We'll even organize a weekend getaway, to keep the spirits up. It's going to be sooo fun!" She winked, leaving the fake eyelash glued to her eye crooked. "How does that sound, honey?"

A beat passed. *Like fresh hell*, Kaja thought. She opened her mouth to protest, but Robert was quicker, sensing her apprehension.

"You'll have something ready for me by next week," he said in a tone that brooked no argument. "Let me make things simple—fix this, or we'll be forced to cut down on some of the staff." His eyebrows wiggle up his forehead, fighting for their life against the botox. "Are we clear?"

The thing is, Kaja was never good with being put on the spot. Confrontation was something she avoided at all costs. So naturally, she did the most sensible thing she could think of.

"Crystal," she agreed, ignoring the clench in her stomach.

***

A few days later, she lay awake in her room, waiting for sleep to come. The dim light of her bedside lamp cast a mist of orange haze across her room. Even though she was drained, her mind raced. Her usual restlessness had only worsened after visiting Robert's office. The sooner she started looking for a new job, the better—there's no way she could do what Robert asked of her. *I'm a fucking moron*, she thought. *Will I ever grow a damn backbone?* Frustrated, she glanced around her messy room. The quiet of her empty, vacant apartment felt stifling. Whatever could she offer to someone else? A shiver ran through her body. She pulled the cover to her neck, letting the weight of it soothe her. She was so tired of adapting.

Kaja squirmed, nestling herself deeper into the warmth of her bed. Bloated lips, bloody cotton pads, pink, scalpel-thin incisions hidden sneakily into the hairline—the images were swirling behind her eyes as soon as she closed them, making her dizzy. The whirlpool inside her agitated brain was relentless. Soon, Robert and Sandra appeared in the middle of it, merging into each other. *Fix this*, they said in unison, pulling Kaja with them, and soon, she was dizzy, falling into the darkness.

Just as she was on the very brink of sleep, she heard a shuffle in the corner of the room. Kaja let out a sigh, stirring. Ah. It's going to be one of those nights, then.

She stretched her limbs, trying to get comfortable before it started.

Something wet dropped on her cheek. Kaja looked up while she was still able to.

She was on the ceiling this time, head bent at an unnatural angle. They stared at each other in silence, like always, and as the first *hiss* came out, inspiration miraculously struck. Kaja let out a manic laugh. She could barely move her mouth anymore, but it pooled out of her, rumbling through her chest, even as jagged arms surged toward her.

***

A week later, Kaja knocked on Robert's door and dumped a pile of papers and face charts on his table. She fidgeted in her seat as he went through it.

After a while, he finally lifted his head and looked at Kaja.

"We can work with this," he said, his pillow-face grimacing into a smile.

***

It's already dusk when they finally arrive at the foot of the hills. According to the GPS, there's only half an hour left until they reach the lodge. The last stretch of the ride has been quiet, filled only by the soft snores coming from the passenger seat—Tihana dozed off about an hour ago, letting Kaja take in their ambience in peaceful silence. The road started to lead them through a dense, dark forest a while ago. The colorful leaves have mostly fallen down and stuck themselves across the gray, damp road, leaving the trees bare and spindly.

Squinting through the receding light, Kaja notices a sign by the road. *Rest stop*, it reads, giving her the perfect excuse to take a break and enjoy her last moment of calm before they arrive at their hellish destination.

Sure enough, there's a wooden picnic table after a few hundred meters. Thankfully, it's empty—the last thing Kaja wants right now is small talk with some overzealous hiker family, her nerves getting higher with each kilometer they get closer to the lodge. She pulls the car over and gently pokes Tihana's shoulder, but she doesn't stir a bit. After a few shakes, Kaja gives up and gets out of the car.

She stretches her limbs, shoulders rigid from the hours-long drive. The air is crisp and fresh, pinching her cheeks; Kaja inhales deeply, the smell of damp earth filling her lungs. As she walks up to the picnic table, she notices a small path behind it, leading into a pine forest. Coming closer, a faint sound of water gurgling reaches her ears. Kaja itches for a quick walk. She steps out on the path, careful not to slip on the muddy ground. This part of the woods is not as deep—after a minute or two of walking down the track, she's met with a small stream. It's narrow, water rushing down its rock and pebbles, gently sloshing away. Fields of golden maize spread beyond it, still wet from the rain, glistening in the last rays of sunlight.

Kaja lays down the parka tied around her waist and sits on the damp bench. Glancing between the fields spreading in front of her and the hills rising behind her, a primordial sense of insignificance and loneliness flashes through her. A chill runs through her body. She pulls her sweatshirt hood over her head, the warmth of the fuzzy lining comforting her. The safe concrete of the city, the hustle and bustle of its streets feels eons away.

Her phone buzzes in her pocket. A message from Dejan lights up on the screen.

When are you coming? It's getting late, it reads, followed by a couple of wink emojis, and an eggplant one. Kaja groans, stuffing the phone back into her pocket. Oh, how she wished she had an ounce of his brazen self-esteem. She still cringes at the memory of the drunken night they spent together a few weeks ago, after Sandra dragged them all out of the clinic to get some forced, after-work drinks.

Absently, Kaja traces the surface of the bench beneath her, fingers dragging across the damp, rugged wood. There are initials engraved into it, framed by awkwardly etched hearts. Annoyed, she moves her hand to the other side. With a frown, she notices long, deep lines carved into the wood, resembling animal scratches. Unease creeps into her as she throws back a quick glance at the hills. She better stick to the lodge for the weekend. Who knows what kinds of beasts are hidden in the woods: thirsty vampires or chainsaw-wielding madmen; freshly-awoken demonic creatures or stinky, lanky cryptids; a bunch of leather-wearing, fashionable Cenobites, or, God forbid, the worst of all, that wretched—

A sudden rustle behind her makes her jolt.

"Kaja, where are you?" Tihana yells. She can hear the woman slipping on the mud, cursing and whimpering her way through the path. After a few moments, Kaja shows mercy.

"Over here!" she shouts. She can't keep from smirking as Tihana's panicked face emerges from the bushes. "Did you think the *hicks* got me?"

"Oh *ha ha*, very funny." Tihana flips her off, looking at her muck-stained boots with disdain. She settles down next to Kaja and pulls out a coffee thermos from her bag.

After taking a sip, she nudges Kaja to do the same, and Kaja gladly accepts her offer, wondering if her bag is an endless supply of drinks and snacks.

For a while, they sit in silence, passing the thermos back and forth.

"I really do hope your top secret project puts us on the map again," Tihana says once they've finished the drink. "It would be a shame if we were to close down. I love squeezing pimples."

Kaja huffs. "It's not a top-secret project," she dismisses with a sigh. "It's just a normal one." She kicks herself internally. For all her grumpy attitude and antisocial tendencies, she really hates lying.

Tihana rustles through her bag. "Well, Robert sure made it seem like it. Why else would he have called us to this fancy lodge for you to tell us about it?" She pulls out her lip balm, applying it with a smack, before fishing out her electric cigarette.

Because he likes to spend money he doesn't have, Kaja wants to reply, but settles for her signature mute shrug before she stands up and walks to the stream.

Tihana takes a puff. "Well, whatever it is, I hope it works. It's been depressing lately at work. I only get to pop like, *three* pimples a *day*."

"Yeah," Kaja agrees, crouching down. "The pandemic was harsh on many businesses." Her reflection is wobbly and blurry, shredded into pieces by the pebbles. She skims her hand across the surface, feeling the cold seep through her palm.

"It wasn't the pandemic, though," Tihana says between the gurgles of her cigarette. "It had something to do with Butcher."

Kaja frowns, turning back to look at her. "Butcher?"

"You haven't heard?"

"Heard what?" Kaja urges.

Tihana stares at her manicured nails. "I don't know the details, but I heard he did something bad. After it happened, we lost half of our customers. Sandra got hired to help us save face, but apparently, word spread regardless. That's why we're so broke."

Kaja considers this for a moment. A man nicknamed *Butcher*, doing something bad? Who would've guessed. Tihana joins her by the stream, picking at the little rocks along its edge.

"Must've been pretty awful, if it scared the customers away," Kaja says after a while. "Robert never said anything?"

"Nope," Tihana replies. "Your guess is as good as mine. Did he do a botched boob job? Give someone flabby asscheeks? Beats me." She throws a pebble at the stream. They watch it disappear into the whirling water with a dull *splash*. "You know they never give me any details, or trust me with anything serious," she divulges quietly. A tinge of sadness laces through her usual carefree tone. "I'm just there to pop pimples, after all."

Her shoulder hunched. She looks like a kicked puppy, and goddamn, Kaja's shit at comforting people.

"That's not true," she offers awkwardly, standing up, "you also do lash extensions and eyebrow microblading." She tries to give an encouraging smile, stiffly shifting on her feet. "You're skilled at what you do. If you don't feel appreciated, you could always quit and start your own business, you know? Blow them off. It's their loss."

Suddenly, Tihana perks up, jumping in front of Kaja. "Kaja, you big softy!" she coos, bumping their shoulders together. The grin on her face is blinding, bright and shiny like the goddamn sun, and Kaja wonders how it's so easy for some people to smile like that. "I wish I was more like you. You're so unbothered, like you don't care what people think about you."

Kaja laughs glumly, shaking her head. "I care," she replies. "I care way more than I should." Before Tihana could open her mouth again, Kaja turns around and heads back to the path.

"C'mon, let's get going," she says. "We're almost there."

The hills loom in front of them, seemingly endless in the dark cloak of dusk.

Chapter 2

IT'S ALREADY PITCH BLACK when they finally pull up to the lodge. Sandra's there to greet them, waving excitedly—smothered by a beige fur coat and with her long, blond ponytail, she looks like an overgrown shih tzu begging to be let out for a walk. Kaja blinks. She wishes she had turned into a flesh-eating zombie after all.

"Welcome to our little slice of heaven for the next few days," Sandra chirps, pointing excitedly toward the lodge. The countless bracelets around her wrist are dangling like chimes, their jingle piercing in the stillness around them.

For once, Kaja actually has to agree with Sandra: the lodge is a two-story summer house built from wood and glass, blending perfectly with the surrounding woods. It's unobtrusively luxurious and quaint at the same time, with a small yard to the side and a fairy light-adorned path leading to a small viewpoint. If she knew the inside wasn't filled with a bunch of obnoxious people, Kaja would find it quite serene.

Sandra cackles her signature hyena laugh. "Wait until you see the hot tub in the back." She beams, ushering the both of them inside.

Kaja and Tihana are the last ones to arrive—once they dump the suitcases in their shared bedroom upstairs, they join the rest of the crew in the big, open-spaced living room. There's a wooden, Zagorje-typical carving on one of the walls, depicting a pastoral, wine-filled gathering.

Hicks, Kaja sees Tihana mouthing to her.

They sit next to Dejan and Butcher on the couch. Kaja's intent on ignoring Dejan's stupid smirking glance he keeps throwing her way, instead watching Robert top their glasses with his frozen face like the world's most dispassionate waiter. Sandra's across the room, leaning against the massive dining table, smiling and blinking like a haunted antique doll.

Three days, Kaja's thinking again, and swallows down a whine.

"Well, now that we're all here," Robert says, "let's make a toast." He raises his glass. "To Beautifully Beautiful," he announces, and the others croon after him, slurping the wine.

"To Beautifully Beautiful," Kaja murmurs before chugging down the drink. A drop of red falls to the white couch, slowly spreading its crimson edges.

***

Dinner is a cold and stale charcuterie board served on a platter. Kaja chews on a sinewy slice of cured meat. According to Robert, the lodge's owner prepared it himself, leaving it as a sign of welcome.

"He said it was from a deer he caught himself in the woods," Robert explains.

Butcher grunts in approval, stabbing another few slices off the platter. "Good meat," he rumbles, scratching at his teeth with a stubby finger, "but not enough fat."

Dejan hums, inspecting a piece of it stabbed on his fork. "Well, we're in the middle of the woods. Maybe we can hunt down something that's better suited to your refined taste, huh?"

Butcher snorts, almost choking in the process. “Deal,” he barks out through a barely chewed mouthful, and Kaja can’t stop the shivers running down her spine. She doesn’t know what makes her more queasy: the supposed dark secret he’s been harboring or his atrocious table manners.

Once the platters are cleared out, Robert winks at Kaja. She forces a smile, picking at her dry cuticles underneath the table.

“As you all know, we didn’t come here just for pleasure,” he announces, standing up. “Our dear colleague Kaja has been working on something interesting these past few weeks.”

He urges Kaja to stand up with his constipated glare.

“A challenging few years are behind us,” Robert muses. “Some of you may have noticed that business has been a bit slower than usual. We had our challenges in the past, but somehow, we got through them—and we’ll make sure to keep doing so.”

Kaja steals a glance at Butcher, but he’s not looking at anyone, fumbling with a bottle of beer and a bottle opener. How he performed allegedly successful surgeries for more than thirty years, Kaja will never know. Eventually, Dejan puts him out of his misery, grabbing the bottle and popping it open. Robert clears his throat, looking even more jaded than usual.

“As I was saying,” he continues, “it’s been tough, lately. Being a cold, hard realist, I’m not the one to deny it. But with a little push, Kaja thought of a wonderful idea that might help us get back on track.” He turns to Kaja, who does her best not to give him the stink eye.

“Please, Kaja,” Robert says, “tell us about your project.”

Kaja's about as taut as a bowstring. Five pairs of eyes look expectantly at her, making her stomach cramp. She feels like she's back in high school, presenting in front of her gossipy classmates. With a deep breath, Kaja retrieves a folder from her bag and takes out a stack of papers. Her jaw feels rigid as a bear trap, but she somehow forces it open. *Clink-clank*, it screeches.

"Well, ah, thank you Robert," she begins awkwardly, words coming out strenuous, like they're being pulled out by pliers. She's always hated presenting, let alone something so personal.

They don't know, she reminds herself, *so relax*.

"So, uh..." She clears her throat. "I'm sure most of you are aware of the tale of Babaroga."

A bout of laughter spreads around the table—of course it does—but Tihana shushes it with a hiss before giving Kaja two enthusiastic thumbs-ups. For all the grief Kaja gave her in the car earlier, she's really grateful Tihana's here.

"It's a short one, I guess—there isn't really much to her story," she continues. "She's a horned, old lady who likes to steal and eat naughty children. She's also known not to be... traditionally good looking."

"You mean ugly?" Butcher interrupts, stifling a burp.

Sandra drums her acrylic nails against the table. "Conventionally unattractive, Butcher, please," she says in her HR voice.

Kaja pauses for a moment, fidgeting with the edges of the folder. "Yes, she's a conventionally unattractive woman," she confirms. "But is that all she is? What if there's more to her than we thought? After all, we don't even know who Babaroga really is, or how she came to be."

She opens the folder and pulls out a bunch of papers, sliding them across the table. Images of horned creatures are soon splayed in front of them, ranging from impressionable sketches made in coal to digitally rendered drawings. The faces vary, depicting Babaroga in various states: some are muted and obtusely sinister, while others are outlandishly monstrous. One could easily mistake this for a work critique session in an art class. Very campy.

Kaja lifts one of the drawings from the table. "All we know is how she's portrayed. Sagging skin, a big, bumpy nose, hairy moles, and a hunched back. But what if..."

She stops for a moment, eyes glued to the drawings. Her eyes blink a few times as her nails come to pinch her finger.

"What if Babaroga's just one of us, trying to fit in, to lead a normal life?" She pulls out another set of drawings. Unlike the sketches of Babaroga, they all look the same—smooth, poreless skin; brilliantly white teeth; plump lips and a small, dainty nose.

"For better or worse, we live in a visual world. We can all say that looks don't matter, but they do." Kaja picks at the face charts with sweaty fingers. "We also live in a busy world, where not much time is left for vanity. Isn't it draining to think about yourself constantly? To think about your skin, your body, about how people perceive you. Nobody wants to be singled out, to be gawked at." Her breathing's becoming winded, and she has to remind herself that this isn't one of her dreams. "We have a lot of procedures at our clinic. When we do those surgeries, we enhance or correct the issues that bother people. It's usually minor—a bit of filler, maybe a nose job.

But what about those who want a one-eighty? Who wants to reinvent themselves? What if we could offer a permanent lift to that struggle?"

Dejan hums, leaning back in his chair. "Ah, so noble," he coos, but Kaja ignores him, pushing ahead.

"Say we make a treatment—a treatment for people who feel like that. We include a full face and body transformation. Starting small, with some filler and botox. Then, a brow tuck, maybe some implants, if they're needed. Then a nose job, a breast lift or an augmentation. And in the end, a liposuction to round it up."

She pulls out the last stack of papers from her folder.

"This," she says, handing copies around the table, "is not just a make-over. We offer beauty, of course, but we also offer peace. The core of this treatment is the right to choose—we can choose beauty, choose serenity. We have some control over ourselves, about how other people perceive us. And it starts with the way we look."

Kaja closes her mouth, trying to ease her breathing. Her legs tremble like she just ran a marathon.

Sandra, though, appears to be having the time of her life, frantically typing on her laptop. "That's brilliant," she mutters, "it will look so good in a LinkedIn post." She turns to the others. "So, what do we think?"

"Bye-Bye, Babaroga," Dejan reads, glancing at the papers splayed across the table. "Very clever." He purses his lips, shifting his eyes over to Kaja. "I like it," he says with a smug smile, "but what about the horn? Will the horn disappear once the treatment is done?"

Kaja was wrong, before—she feels like she's back in *elementary* school.

"The horn is not that important," she replies with a pinched expression. "It's just a metaphor."

"Oh, I'd say that *the horn* is very important!" he presses on, scoffing dramatically. "I would say its *prick* is a matter of life or death, don't you think?"

Butcher snorts beside him, meaty shoulders twitching. Before he can grunt something crude, Robert stands up and tugs warningly at one of his flabby ears, before heading toward the fridge.

"Well, we can contemplate that some other day," he says. "Tomorrow we'll talk about potential candidates who could showcase the treatment, but now, I'd like to raise a second toast."

The loud pop of the champagne bottle startles Kaja. A few moments later, a glass flute is shoved into her hand.

"To our upcoming campaign," Robert says, "Bye-Bye, Babaroga!"

"Bye-Bye, Babaroga!" the others chant in return, but Kaja goes straight for her glass, draining it down.

***

A few bottles later, Kaja sneaks out for a cigarette. Plodding through the muddy path, she heads toward the soft, orange light post that's shining by the viewpoint.

Inside, the party's starting to quiet down. Tihana went upstairs a while ago, explaining she needed her 'beauty sleep', and Butcher never got that far, snoring away in the armchair. Robert and Sandra were sitting on the couch, pretending to listen to Dejan prattle on about the pros and cons of porcelain veneers. *So* fun.

The hills are spread beneath her, merging into foggy plains in the distance. It's eerily quiet here, the only noise coming from the house. The lights of the surrounding villages are far away and dim, their mute glow shining in the dark mist. Before she could light up a cigarette, she hears footsteps approaching her.

It's Dejan, holding two glasses of wine. Kaja groans internally.

"I thought the party's over," she replies, but accepts the glass. Her throat still feels prickly from all the talking she did earlier.

The corner of Dejan's lips quirks up. "Well, maybe the party moved to a more intimate setting." He sits down next to Kaja, spreading his legs like a frog. "I liked your presentation," he continues, placing his hand on Kaja's thigh, and oh, she doesn't want to handle this right now.

"What's the deal with Robert and Butcher?" she asks, trying to distract him. The hand on her thigh stills.

Dejan clears his throat and takes a sip of wine. "Why do you ask?"

Kaja shrugs. "No particular reason," she replies carefully. "They've known each other for quite some time, right?"

"Well, yeah," he confirms, "he and Robert were college friends."

"They've been through thick and thin together." There's a question behind her statement, and while Dejan is many things, he's not as unperceptive as Kaja would like to think he is. He turns to her, legs spreading even wider, pushing her uncomfortably close to the edge of the bench. What a gentleman.

"Look, I shouldn't be saying this to you, but hell, I'm becoming quite fond of you." Kaja wants to smack his dumb face, but decides on an encouraging nod.

"Butcher had a small... indiscretion a few years ago. He fucked up. Actually, he fucked up a lot, but the issue got resolved. His record is clean, if you were wondering."

"You mean, his record was *wiped* clean."

"Look, even I don't know the details, okay? Accidents happen in the medical world more than we think. He's a solid surgeon. It would be a shame for him to end up behind bars for a simple slipup."

Kaja shrugs again, not convinced. "What an unfortunate nickname, huh?"

"Trust me, the less you know, the better." Dejan shakes his head. "The past is not important. What's important is what's happening right here, right now." He gulps some wine and turns to Kaja, grins his unnaturally white toothy grin into her face. "I think you have something here," he says, "with this whole Babaroga thing. Yes, it's a bit wacky, and those drawings were a bit unhinged, I'm not going to lie, but the thing is you're talented, and so am I. We could work together, I'm sure of it. Why are you fighting this so hard?" Dejan smirks, and unfortunately, Kaja knows exactly what's coming next. "You know who my father is, and I'm about to join the party as well. Don't concern yourself with Robert or Butcher. If you're looking for an easy way up the ladder, your best shot is to stick with me."

Kaja shakes her head. "That's not why I was asking," she huffs.

"I like you," Dejan says, leaning closer. His teeth are fucking blinding. Kaja contemplates blowing smoke in his face. "There's something different about you, something I can't puzzle out. But I like a challenge," he tells her, "and you certainly look like one. Look, at the end of the day, I'm a fucking catch, ok?

The sooner you realize it, the better." With a final squeeze to her thigh, he gets up and walks back to the house.

His touch lingers long after he's gone. What a *fucking catch.* Kaja smokes through half a cigarette pack, but her thigh is still buzzing with unpleasant goosebumps. She knows what he's offering her—a comfortable life, a role to play. A camouflage. It's not so different from the treatment she's come up with, and it's not like she hasn't thought about it, even after their awkward hookup, and yet.

And yet.

She looks at the light of the surrounding villages. When the last one disappears, she heads back into the lodge, sneaking upstairs. Tihana's already fast asleep.

"Do you mind if I leave the light on?" she whispers, but of course, Tihana doesn't rouse. Kaja pulls the cover over her face, wishing for sleep to tackle her quickly.

Chapter 3

KAJA WAS ABOUT EIGHT years old when it first happened.

She never had problems falling asleep before it started. Even when left to her own devices, she wasn't afraid of the dark that enveloped the room as her parents flipped off the switch and bid her goodnight. After all, why should she be? Comfortably nested in her bed, there were so many wonderful things to think about before sleep seized her: the cartoon she'll watch tomorrow morning, the game of hide-and-seek she'll play after school, or the book she will flip through before bed. It appeared that her troubles came out of nowhere, but by the time she'd reached adulthood, Kaja found many excuses for the lack of sleep: she was never pretty enough, never interesting enough. Such a bore. She either talked too little, or cringed at herself when she revealed too much. It seemed like she couldn't do anything right. She was always so unformed, uninteresting, too different from others, and maybe that was exactly why it latched onto her so tightly.

The first time it happened, she burst out of her room as soon as she could move again, running down the hallway to her parents' room. Through ragged sobs, she whimpered about the scary, horned lady who was hiding under her bed, only for them to burst into laughter.

"Sounds like Babaroga's got an eye on you," her mom teased her, causing a fresh surge of tears to swell out of Kaja's eyes.

Babaroga, she thought while violently hiccuping, before weaseling her way under her parents' covers. *What a stupid name.* But then, alarm bells started ringing in her ears. Through a haze of fear, snot and goosebumps, Kaja remembered a story her grandparents told her about a few months ago—a tale of a monstrous, ugly woman you'd never want to cross paths with, called Babaroga. 'Don't be like her,' grandpa had said to her, while grandma nodded wisely beside him. 'That's right,' she continued, looking at Kaja with a grave expression. 'Be a nice girl, Kaja. A *good* girl.'

That night, her dad echoed the sentiment. "Now, be good and go back to sleep," he concluded, rubbing his eyes, "or Babaroga will come back and get you."

And so she did go back to sleep, nestled safely between her parents, the scary, pale woman lurking in her room momentarily forgotten. At that moment, Kaja was convinced the horned creature wouldn't come back to haunt her, because she really was a good girl: she listened to her teachers obediently and got excellent grades without exception. She rarely fought with her parents and never asked them for much. She partook in five extracurricular activities and excelled at all of them. Like any other girl, she had nice, long hair often pinned behind her ears with a butterfly clip, ruffled sundresses, and an album full of colorful stickers that was her pride and joy. Those facts soothed her mind as she was falling back asleep—she was a good girl, a normal girl, just like everyone else, and this won't happen again; not to her, at least.

The nightmares didn't stop, though, as she woke up in the middle of the night a few weeks later with her body stiff and frozen, and two ugly, mud-stained feet poking out under her curtains. What did stop, however, were her late-night, teary-eyed visits to her parents' bedroom.

"You're getting too old for this," her dad rumbled a few years into the routine, waving a dismissive hand at Kaja and the pile of bedding she was dragging with her. Oh, boy. Kaja barely suppressed the pathetic quiver of her lips. Eyes full of tears, she wobbled back to her room like a wounded animal.

She tried to be brave about it. After all, she was twelve—in two years, she'll be starting high school, and last month, her parents let her go to the cinema and watch a horror movie unsupervised, thank you very much. From that point on, she made it through the terrors alone. It's not like anybody was going to help her. Her friends didn't get the severity of her situation. *Dreams are not real*, they said. From their laid-back attitude, Kaja could tell that none of them ever experienced what she was going through, so she just resolved to keep her mouth shut, trying to conceal the fact that she was beginning to be the odd man out.

Kaja tried everything. She talked to the creature, whispered pleas and prayers, negotiated, leveraged, offered, groveled and begged, but it seemed that her desperate attempts only made the monster more vicious. Babaroga knew no reason or logic—just growls and hisses and red-hot terror.

"Why won't you leave me alone?" Kaja would whisper as a horn protruded out of her closet, sharp and ragged, but never got an answer. Which was fine, honestly. It's not like she needed it spelled out anyway.

Actions spoke louder than words, and the creature seemed to tell her, *There is no rest for the wicked*, and the two of them would stay up all night, until the first light of day.

Although her room read more as a torture chamber from *Hellraiser* than a safe haven, Kaja spent most of her time in it, haunting it almost like the creature haunted her. After school was done, she didn't linger much around: she headed straight home, pulled down the blinds, and found solace in books and movies. She liked horror movies the best, and rewatched *The Ring* a hundred times. It was oddly therapeutic. If she went into psychology instead of surgery, she'd be able to write her graduation thesis on herself.

For better or for worse, she'd roam the internet, scrolling through various threads and reading poorly worded comments that would make her pull at her cuticles until they bled. Sometimes, when it was late at night and she could still move her body, she'd jam earphones in her ears and look up things she didn't have the courage to in the daylight. She was always careful, though, to clean her history once she was done.

Out of sight, out of mind.

She studied hard, and aimed to get into Med school. Not that she had any particular interest in it—she just thought that sounded like something a nice, good girl would do. It definitely wasn't something that a weird girl would do, Kaja reasoned. A small flicker of hope pushed her through her teenage years that maybe, when she left her tiny bedroom and this small town, Babaroga wouldn't follow, but lying on the bumpy dorm mattress in Zagreb, she found her neck stiffening and she let out a tired groan.

Nothing got better. It seemed like Babaroga latched herself onto Kaja with a sharp, invisible string, and no matter where Kaja lived, or how she behaved or dressed, she couldn't unknot it. Maybe, even though she was a good person—*a good girl*—there was something dark and foul inside of her, something she wasn't even aware of etched into her bones and weaved through her flesh, and Babaroga smelled it, clung to it, recognized it as her own.

Years later, staring at the ceiling, something struck her. What if she got this all wrong? Maybe, the problem wasn't in Kaja—after all, she'd successfully adapted into society, with her forced smiles, timid nature, pretty clothes, and gel nails. It's not like Babaroga could just go into a salon and request a balayage and a mani-pedi, right? The thought of it amused Kaja, and she would have smiled, if the muscles would have allowed her to. She didn't know much, but she knew of ugliness and shame and constant dread. She knew what it was like to drag something hideous and nasty with you at all times, and she thought she might have come up with a solution.

'Demand and supply,' her boss would say to her a few days later, congratulating her on a job well done.

Her motive for making the treatment was utterly selfish. It was never about beauty, or helping others, or whatever the fuck she'd blabbed about in front of her colleagues—it was about exorcising her own demons, again and again, until she felt better.

What a sneaky, little Mother Teresa she was. Almost as bad as the real one.

She buried the guilt somewhere deep down, without even thinking twice about it. Kaja felt entitled to it, as her life wasn't some heartwarming tale of self love, or a profoundly angsty coming-of-age movie. She knew she wasn't special or important, only good for injecting filler into perfectly normal lips and erasing every sign of aging on women whose frontal lobe wasn't even developed yet, but after years of silent torment, she felt deserving of some goddamn piece.

That's why she sat in Robert's office, a folder full of sketches and unnecessary treatments splayed in front of them, and nodded at his praise.

What a sneaky, little coward she was.

***

Tonight, Kaja wakes up in the dark of the room, although she knows she left her bedside lamp on. Ah, classic Babaroga. She rolls her eyes, savoring the only movement she's able to do at the moment.

She's frozen on her side, facing Tihana's bed, her neck stuck in an uncomfortable position. Kaja waits, blinking at Tihana's dormant form. She glances at the window behind her conked-out roommate. The rustle of the lanky branches against the windowsill is making her tense.

There's still no sign of her yet. Kaja wishes Babaroga would just hurry up and get this done, or by tomorrow, along with some nasty dark circles, she'll have a horrible crick in her neck.

It's quiet in the room, though; the only sound is Tihana's soft snoring. An owl hoots here and there, getting on Kaja's nerves. She waits and waits, limbs glued to the bed. The pale shine of the moonlight is casting a soft veil of blue across the room, making everything seem dreamlike. It would be calming, if it weren't for the painful clench nestled in Kaja's stomach.

Maybe she won't come tonight after all, she considers, but knows that's just wishful thinking. She's beginning to run hot underneath the covers, sweat pooling around her neck.

It would be natural to assume that the impending dread is the worst part of Babaroga's nightly visits—sharp, ragged nails dragging across her skin; the rough, iron grip that leaves bruises gone by morning; the tear of pointed teeth piercing her skin, every time feeling like the first. Of course, the pain is gruesome, but to Kaja, what's worse is the waiting: lying in the dark, unable to move, just anticipating for Babaroga to slither into Kaja's view and bare her teeth. A feeling of utter powerlessness strums through every inch of her body, reminding her that, for the next few hours, she's about to lose all control, and there's no one in this world who can help her.

Finally, something rustles underneath Tihana's bed. Kaja's gaze snaps downward, meeting glowing, ember eyes. A slow growl fills the room and Kaja knows it's about to start.

The ragged, bony horn emerges first, followed by a pair of wrinkly arms. Jagged nails scrape against the wooden floor, and Kaja hates how familiar it sounds. A hiss comes from the dark, and soon, with a swift pull and a snap of bones, Babaroga drags herself from underneath the bed, rising up crooked and cadaverous and wretched as always.

She's smiling at Kaja, standing beside Tihana's bed. She likes to do that before anything else—for a thing like her, it's an appetizer of sorts—and bare her teeth into a big, wide grin, so wide that it reaches her ears and contorts her face in a way that's painful to watch. Kaja's never gotten used to it, and thinks she never will. Years later, it still sends shivers down her spine:

the sharp teeth, the cracked, salivating mouth, the glowing red eyes, wide and bulging, full of impish joy and anticipation for what's to come.

She stares at Kaja like that for quite some time, leering in silence. The smell of her is slowly starting to spread through the room, making the air stinky and thick. Kaja's staring right back at her, a tear sliding from her eyes every now and then—by the time Babaroga finally moves, the pillow is uncomfortably damp underneath Kaja's face.

Babaroga's gangly arms are now reaching slowly to the side. Much to Kaja's horror, she bends and drags a torn fingernail across the smooth, plump surface of Tihana's cheek, dipping into the soft skin, and enjoys the way Kaja's eyes widen in mute frenzy. Then, with a fracturing, alacritous motion, she jumps at the wall on all fours, with her long, black hair whirling across the room and her body contorting in impossible angles. She shrieks, piercing and ear splitting, before disappearing from Kaja's view.

The scream leaves a tense silence in its wake. By now, Kaja's boiling under the covers, smothered by the heat and fear likewise. There's a hushed, uncanny shuffling coming from above her, underneath her, behind her, claw like fingernails scratching the walls, the floor. The sulphury, rotten stench is becoming stronger, filling out Kaja's nostrils and making it hard to breathe, as if to say: *Yes, you're about to suffocate, and yes, there isn't a thing that you can do about it.* She hopes that she won't barf or piss the bed, as she sometimes does. It would be tricky to explain to Tihana in the morning—*Babaroga made me do it, I swear,* she'd plead, watching Tihana scrunch her nose in disgust like she did when she smelled the cow shit on their ride to Kalnik.

The bed dips behind her. Kaja can smell the foulness of Babaroga's breath, the stink of the dirt hidden in the folds of her unwashed body. Wet, ragged wheezes graze her cheek. The covers are peeled away from her, dragging slowly across her stiff body, leaving her exposed. The cold air clings uncomfortably to her clammy skin, pinches her sweaty neck. Babaroga cackles in joy, but Kaja barely hears it, with her ears buzzing like a nest of hornets.

A bony hand wraps around her neck. It's calloused and rough against her skin, the hold tightening with every second. Kaja looks at Tihana peacefully sleeping, and thinks, like she did many times in her life, *I wish I were like everybody else.*

And then, pointy teeth sink into the soft flesh of her neck, and she knows nothing else at the moment, other than pain.

Chapter 4

TIHANA'S ALARM WAKES KAJA up in the morning. Kaja groans as the sound of it blasts through the room, jabbing at her ears. It's a familiar tune, but she's still too groggy to recognize it.

Kaja swings from the bed and stretches her body, feeling the floor's coolness against her bare feet. It seeps into her skin, makes her shudder. Things like these have always been a part of her post-nightmare ritual: plastering something hot or cold against her skin, squeezing her fists, scraping her nails against her forearms. She'll do whatever it takes to distract herself, make her stiff body uncurl and come back to her.

"I'm in control," she whispers and pinches her wrist, letting the sting pull her away from the afterimages dancing in front of her eyes.

Outside, the rain is pouring, thumping heavily against the window glass. The alarm's still going off—Madonna's *Hung Up*, Kaja finally acknowledges. She's not really thrilled at the groovy shrill of the synth first thing in the morning. There was enough shrilling done last night. After calling Tihana's name multiple times, Kaja woozily pads to the other side of the room and gently smacks her colleague's drooling face with a pillow.

"Sorry," Tihana mumbles, clumsily snoozing the alarm. "I could sleep through a literal carnage."

Kaja only grunts in response. That's probably true.

She looks at Tihana snuggling back against her covers, and thinks about Babaroga poking her rosy cheek with a rotten finger. Involuntarily, Kaja pinches her skin again before she heads to their shared bathroom, splashing her face with icy water until it's nice and cold and numb. *It's a dream*, she reminds herself, *it's only a fucking dream*, but the painful crick in her neck is telling her: *so what if it is?*

The song goes off again, muted through the bathroom door.

Every little thing that you say or do, I'm hung up, I'm hung up on you, it sings, and Kaja sticks her face under the spray again.

***

Tihana barges into the bathroom a few minutes later, pushing past Kaja with a long sigh. She doesn't seem fazed by Kaja's half-dressed state or her complaints about privacy.

"I look like a mess," Tihana whines and plops a huge cosmetic case on the sink. Kaja shoots her an exasperated look. Tihana doesn't look like a mess at all—on the contrary, she looks like an angelic creature, with her fresh, shiny skin and soft hair charmingly tousled by sleep. Next to her, Kaja just feels like death warmed over, reaching for the concealer to cover the dark circles under her eyes, and blush to pat down her pale, grayish skin. She wishes she could use makeup as a form of self-expression, just like the drag queens she most definitely doesn't watch on YouTube, but alas; her makeup kit is only a camouflage, meant to signalize that she's just a nice, normal girl, a girl with long lashes, rosy cheeks, and glossy lips. She pulls on a nice, boring cashmere sweater, to get that point across further. It's a performance she's been doing for years. A cookie-cutter fantasy.

As Tihana applies what appears to be her tenth face cream, Kaja finds their morning routines eerily similar. Gel cleanser, exfoliator, serum number one, serum number two, face cream, sunscreen, eye cream: the sound of tube-squeezing and skin-smacking is filling up the bathroom. After profusely dabbing all of the products into the skin, Tihana fishes out a roller and starts to massage her cheeks and forehead.

What an elaborate regime, only to end up looking almost the same—Kaja stifles a laugh at the decadent, systematic procedure-like routine going on beside her. The urge to laugh dies down, though, once she remembers she's no better. The whole thing is actually really depressing. She's sure that Butcher and Dejan are still snoring away in their room, unbothered about face mists, retinol treatments or antiaging face massages.

Once she's finally done with her skincare, Tihana stops crowding Kaja at the sink and sits back at the edge of the bathtub, applying her makeup with the help of a small pocket mirror.

"So, you and Dejan," Tihana starts. "What's going on there?" She glides some lip gloss on her lips and smacks them together before blowing Kaja a kiss in the mirror. "I saw him cozying up to you yesterday. Anything to share?"

"Not really," Kaja replies, but with her mouth full of toothpaste, it comes out like a foamy grumble.

Tihana seems to understand her, though, putting down her gloss with a frown. "Why? I mean, he's good-looking, has money, *and* a career. What more could you ask for?" When she's met with a disinterested shrug, she continues to prattle away, pulling her hair back in a ponytail. "What? Is he also not your *type*? Well, I guess he can be a bit sleazy, now that I think about it. Tried to get in my pants, once or twice. He finally backed off when I told him my boyfriend's a Krav Maga instructor." She chuckles and clicks her tongue. "I mean, he wasn't really a Krav Maga instructor. He also wasn't, uh, real—I kind of made him up."

Kaja snickers, imagining Dejan getting trampled down by Tihana's imaginary hunk of a boyfriend: this is a visualization she could get behind, not that she would ever tell that to Sandra.

Behind her, Tihana continues her one-sided conversation. "I guess that someone could be the whole package, but you still couldn't make yourself like them." She stops for a moment, giving Kaja a chance to respond, but Kaja's still fantasizing about Dejan getting smacked around. Maybe the day didn't start so bad after all, even as the downpour outside keeps getting stronger. Tihana clears her throat. "You know I wouldn't care, right?" she says, her tone suddenly uncharacteristically somber, and Kaja stops her brushing.

Their eyes meet in the mirror, but Kaja averts them quickly—suddenly, the makeup-stained sink is the most interesting thing in the world, demanding her undivided attention.

"I wouldn't care if you don't like Dejan," Tihana continues, terribly gently. It only manages to agitate Kaja, who can't bear the thought of being so damn transparable. "You know, if you happen to—"

The soft hair on Kaja's neck stands up like she's a feral, hissy cat. "I don't know what you're talking about," she grumbles on instinct, cutting Tihana short. Tihana's eyes are burning holes into her back, making her shoulders tense in discomfort. She's still as a statue, almost as still as she was yesterday, glued down to the mattress. That annoying crick in her neck isn't helping either.

"Are you sure you don't?"

"Yes," Kaja spews forcibly, foam spluttering all over the bathroom mirror. "I'm sure." Somehow, she manages not to choke herself around a mouthful of toothpaste.

A strike of thunder pierces the taut silence.

"Okay, Miss Broody," Tihana says eventually. "I just wanted to lay it out there, for future references." She struts out of the bathroom, leaving Kaja cemented in front of the foam-defiled sink, the thunder and echoes of their conversation raging inside of her head like the squall outside.

Kaja stalls in the bathroom for quite some time in hopes that Tihana heads downstairs, but once she finally emerges, Tihana is sitting on her bed, scrolling on her phone and puffing her vanilla-scented electric cigarette. She raises her eyebrows at Kaja and heads for the door, playfully punching her shoulder in the process.

"Ready when you are, slowpoke," she jests and flashes a grin at Kaja, and Kaja can do nothing other than follow her downstairs.

Walking behind Tihana, a rush of fondness washes over Kaja. Maybe—occasionally; at times; once in a while—having an irritating little sister around isn't that bad after all.

***

"Brainstorming!" Sandra exclaims as they're all seated around the table.

No one seems to share her enthusiasm. Butcher's draining a can of beer, even though it's barely noon.

He unsuccessfully tries to keep a burp down before opening another one. Robert and Dejan are glancing longingly at the window, looking like they'd rather be caught in the actual storm. Kaja fidgets with her cuticles, resisting the urge to pull at them. Tihana's the only one who looks like she's actually having a good time, nibbling on cheese and sourdough bread with fervor.

Sandra brings her laptop to the table, her stilettos thumping against the wooden floor. She purses her pink lips. "As Kaja kindly explained to us yesterday," she chirps, "we need a candidate who will perfectly showcase the Bye-Bye, Babaroga treatment. I took the liberty of doing a little research myself." Sandra throws a mischievous wink at Kaja as she turns the screen toward the others. Kaja takes a generous gulp of her coffee and braces herself. She has a hunch this will be difficult to digest.

The next few hours are spent flicking through pictures of various women, each of them receiving a background voiceover by Sandra, listing their influence, social media numbers, reach, and target audience.

"*Everything* is sales", Sandra explains with a serious face, pointing a French-tipped nail at a picture of a woman enjoying a croissant.

Butcher and Dejan seem to have a good time after all. That doesn't come as a surprise, as this is exactly the type of activity they like the best: spewing their poorly worded opinions with unmatched gusto. Robert occasionally chimes in. Tihana just squirms in her seat for the most part, snacks abandoned.

Nobody seems to fit the description. Too young or too old; too fat or too skinny; not enough social media presence or not the right *kind* of social media presence—nobody satisfies their refined criteria.

"How's it this hard to find an ugly woman?" Butcher mutters, looking uncharacteristically morose.

As they finally reach the last slide, Kaja's exhausted. She's currently on her third cup of coffee, her heart beating in her chest like a drum, but her energy is lower than it's been in months. *Vultures*, she thinks as she glances between Robert, Sandra, Dejan, and Butcher arguing over the last potential candidate.

Across the table, Dejan throws his hands up in defeat. "They're all too pretty," he concludes with frustration. "We need someone with a proper horse face or, at least, for the love of God, some buck teeth. Someone who's actually hideous, you know?"

Sandra clears her throat. "What you're trying to say is, we need someone more unconventionally looking," she informs him in her monotone HR voice. "Nobody is *hideous*, of course!"

"Of course," echoes Robert in reconciliation, "except for those who are." He looks at one of Kaja sketches lying on the table. "If we only had the real deal, it'd be perfect."

"Kaja, what do you think?" Sandra asks. "Does she exist?"

Thinking about the creature crawling around her room last night, Kaja wants to scream and laugh at the same time. For once, she agrees with her boss—it really would be perfect, if the creature were to magically appear for everyone to see.

"I'm sure she does," she replies instead, feeling the ghost of Babaroga's nightmarish grip against her neck. "We just haven't found her yet."

Underneath the table, her hands lie against her stomach. It started cramping a while ago, clenching anxiously with each slide they passed.

She was right. This was, indeed, rather difficult to digest.

***

By nightfall they're all drunk, except for Tihana, who wisely went off to get her beauty sleep long before their 20th bottle of wine was popped open. The formal aspect of their team building morphed seamlessly into an alcohol-fueled frenzy: Butcher and Dejan are sitting at the table, giggling maniacally like a couple of schoolboys as they rummage through Kaja's face charts with a pencil in their hands, while Sandra and Robert are huddled together in the armchair, moon-eyeing each other, clearly not bothered to conceal their affair any longer.

Kaja's drinking her final glass of wine for the night. Given her company, she's as relaxed as she can get, nestled on the couch at a safe distance from the others. The room spins a bit with each blink she takes, and the lights are a bit fuzzy—she's way more drunk than she planned to be, but she had to make it through the day somehow. The storm finally began to wind down a while ago, leaving only a quiet, pleasant murmur of drizzle behind.

When Robert extracts himself from Sandra's perfumed limbs and joins the guys at the table, Kaja knows her peace is about to get disrupted. Before she can bolt upstairs, Sandra staggers over, clumsy strutting in her high heels, looking like a disoriented stork.

"This rain is a tragedy," she announces and plops down next to Kaja. "I wanted to have a relaxing soak in the hot tub, but the weather's been miserable the whole day. Tomorrow's my last chance. I'll get into that tub even if I drown in there."

Kaja hums affirmatively, downing the rest of her glass. "Everything's possible if you set your mind to it," she imparts on Sandra, feeling generous. She really is drunk.

"Exactly!" Sandra nods, clasping her hands. "You're starting to get it." She tops their glasses and clinks them together. Kaja lets her, because Sandra's hogwash is way more fun when she's inebriated.

"Is that so? I was starting to fret I wasn't fitting in," Kaja replies with false disquiet. The alcohol's making her more flippant than she usually would be, but Sandra's too drunk to notice. She pins Kaja with a sloshed, cross-eyed stare, before leaning over and smothering Kaja with her booze breath.

"Did you know that Robert didn't want to hire you at first?" Sandra whispers confidentially. "It was nothing personal, of course. You're a good doctor, as good as any. It's just that...well. Please, don't take this the wrong way, but you didn't exactly fit with our company values. Like, visually. Or character wise." She hiccups. "Actually, you're kind of a downer."

"Uh," Kaja says, "right." *Miss Broody*, is what Tihana said to her this morning. Sandra's finger comes to poke at her chest. *Ouch*, Kaja thinks. Almost as sharp as Babaroga's.

"Yes, he didn't want to hire you, but I saw something in you, something special. I mean, *sure*, you could lose a few pounds, and that hair—" she frowns "—it could do with some anti-frizz treatments. Your attitude can also be a bit depressing, with the way you mope around the clinic like a sad weirdo. But that's your appeal, you know? You are an unpolished jewel—so raw and unformed. It's kind of rare to find someone like you, nowadays. So *raw* and *real* and *sad*.

I looked at you, and said to myself, 'Sandra, you could change her, help reach her full potential.' And I did! You just needed a little push, that's all."

Kaja blinks. "Sure," she offers for lack of a better response. "Thanks for the, uh, little push, Sandra."

Kaja woozily stands up, ready to retreat upstairs and sleep off this interaction, but Sandra pulls her back down and locks their hands together with the strength of their newfound camaraderie.

"Let me give you some advice," Sandra says with a serious face. A few beats pass as she actually does so. "Don't work smart, work hard." She frowns. "No, what I meant to say was, don't work *hard*, work *smart*." She looks over at the table with a sheepish expression. "We are not like them, are we?" she huffs, gesturing at the guys. "We're fragile, unprotected. We need to work around the system a bit. The quicker you learn that, the better."

"That's not very feminist of you, Sandra," Kaja begrudges her, unable to help herself. She takes another sip of wine, amused by Sandra's flabbergasted expression.

"Oh, feminist *this*, feminist *that*!" Sandra squawks, her jewelry clinking like a wind chime. "Do you know what paid for this beautiful bracelet, huh? For this wonderful getaway? For that magnificent hot tub? No? Well, let me tell you—it certainly wasn't *feminism*." She scoffs and puckers her wine-stained lips. "The truth is, Kaja, that we can't fend for ourselves. It's a man's world out there, and we need to play a certain way to survive. Next time your precious *feminism* tells you that we're equal, think again," she says mockingly. "I mean, just look at Butcher, right? His negligence killed some poor girl, and did he ever pay for that? Did he feel the consequences of his actions? Like hell he did. I made sure of that."

Kaja freezes mid-gulp, eyes wide. *I called it*, is her first thought. *A man nicknamed Butcher, doing something bad?* rings in her ear so loud she has to frown in discomfort.

"Killed?" she asks dumbly. Suddenly, the room starts spinning, more and more, and she has to concentrate hard on keeping Sandra's face static.

The swirling head barks out a laugh, loud and manic. "Oh, don't look so shocked," Sandra says. "*Yes*, it was tragic, and *sure*, it was awful, but it could've happened to anybody. What would you know? You and Tihana only squeeze pimples, pump up some lips, and break a nose here and there. Medical accidents happen *all* the time. You just don't hear about it. That's why Robert hired me, after all—because I'm so good at my job."

Kaja opens and closes her mouth, words rising and then dying out in her throat. She's having a hard time following the information, but on the other hand, things make perfect sense. After all, a butcher butchers, right? The couch is starting to get uncomfortable, and Kaja squirms, restless, as a wave of nausea hits her.

Next to her, Sandra lets out a long sigh, looking over at Butcher. "He got distracted, drained too much, and a poor soul got snuffed," she continues, now a bit maudlin, "and yes, it's very *sad* and very *tragic*, but we paid good money to make it go away. The parents might've lost a daughter, but they sure as hell won the lottery. That's what we, in psychology, like to call looking at the glass half full."

Kaja stands up abruptly. "I need to pee," she says and heads to the toilet, ignoring Sandra's disapproving caw. Her legs shake as she passes the guys on her way, uncomfortably aware of Dejan's smirk, and the questioning stare Robert shoots at Sandra.

She barges into the bathroom and leans against the door. Back in the living room, Butcher snorts like a pig, probably choking on some leftover dried meat, and she wishes she could go back to a time when she thought that was his biggest crime.

A succession of heavy knocks raps at the door and she jumps away. Dejan quietly slides in and locks the door behind him. He takes a step toward Kaja, licking his lips.

"Here you are," he drawls with a suggestive wink, as if Kaja didn't witness enough disturbing things today.

She pulls rigidly at the neckline of her sweater, struggling for air. "Now's really not a good time," she informs him, but Dejan just smirks, backing her against the tile.

"Always so tense," he muses as his hands drag up against her side. "If you want to release some of this tension, I can think of a few ways to make that happen."

Kaja swats Dejan's wandering hands away, irritated. His dumb cologne is making her more nauseous.

"Look, that night won't happen again," she tells him, fighting the urge to barf Regan MacNeil style all over his expensive polo shirt. "We're colleagues. It wouldn't be professional."

His hands don't waver much, though, as they find her shoulder a few seconds later, holding her in place. *Just a little push*, Kaja imagines Sandra's voice.

"All the more reason," he says in a hushed tone. "Think about it. If we combine our strengths, there's no stopping us—you're smart and have good ideas, and I'm a freaking hotshot. Dentistry's all the craze right now. Veneers are the future, baby, and you know that my father's—"

"Yeah, yeah, your father's in the *freaking* party," Kaja cuts him off, not baring to listen to him a second longer.

The walls of the room seem to be shrinking, and *god*, she'll end up being squished flat against him, unable to breathe between his smothering limbs, if she doesn't get out right now. She tries to push past him, but he remains unmoving, solid like a brick wall against her trembling body.

Dejan shakes his head, amused pity written across his face. "You're almost thirty, you can't stall forever," he says. "The old clock is ticking, so please, spare us of this hard-to-get schtick. I want you, and I always get what I want in the end. Just think about it. You, me, together. The sky's going to be the limit, baby."

Kaja barks out a laugh. "You're spending too much time around Sandra," she snaps at him. "You sound like a cheap self-help coach."

"And you sound like a stuck-up, frigid *bitch*," he bites out in return, spittle landing all over Kaja's cheeks.

"Let me go!" she yells back at him and pushes at his chest with all the strength she can muster. Dejan finally steps back, probably more due to fear of a sexual misconduct accusation than respect for her private space, but Kaja doesn't care. She bolts to the door, pulling shakily at the doorknob.

"Fuck you," she spits back at him.

Dejan only shrugs. "Well, soon, hopefully," he says, patting down his crumpled shirt, "once you finally sort out your goddamn priorities."

Kaja stumbles into the hallway, clenching her fists like she's just finished a boxing match, which is a fair comparison, really. The tension running through her body feels unbearable—she has to clear her head, has to move away from this stinking lodge this very second or something inky and ugly and gaping will swallow her whole, so she grabs her parka and bolts through the back door toward the forest.

Damp air fills her lungs as she follows the narrow path into the dark. The rain's finally stopped, but a storm's still raging inside of Kaja's head. Robert's shameless blackmail, Sandra's idiotic blabbering; Dejan's arrogant smile, and those nasty, roaming hands. And finally, Butcher's alleged 'snuffing of a poor soul', as Sandra nicely put it. *Birds of a feather flock together*, Kaja's poor, drunk brain's screaming at her, and she most certainly doesn't want to be anywhere near those birds, thank you very much. Tears pool in the corner of her eyes, stinging in the cold air.

Her head's spinning, thoughts jumping violently from one to another. The hyena laughs, the burps, the ugly polo shirts and veneers, and the murder all merge into one freakish, shadowy beast chasing her further into the forest. The wine in her stomach sloshes back and forth as she stomps gracelessly through the dark, but she doesn't stop, not even when the ground underneath starts to feel like cotton candy, all soft and round and bouncy. She can barely see anything, but she's confident that if she turned on the flashlight on her phone, the bright light would be too much for her spinny head and poor stomach and she'd end up projectile vomiting all over the trees and bushes and shrubs, and if there was a time and place to projectile vomit, it was back in that bathroom and all over Dejan's ugly shirt.

Kaja's not surprised when something catches on her foot and she trips, twisting her ankle painfully in the process. If she were to be honest, as she dives headfirst into the cold, muddy ground, she almost feels relieved.

At last, some peace and quiet, is what she's thinking before her head collides with something sharp and solid, and everything goes comfortably black.

Chapter 5

SOMETIMES, THE NIGHTMARES KAJA has leave the four walls of her bedroom.

She dreams of the playground where she used to play as a kid, or the bedroom of her childhood best friend who she hasn't spoken to in years. From time to time, Babaroga will follow her to her high school classroom or a dimly lit cafe she used to visit during college. The scenery may vary, but the ending's always the same.

Right now, she's back in her hometown, walking to the outskirts, headphones jammed into her ears. Her friend is waiting for her there, on a shoddy field next to the woods. They started coming there when they turned fourteen, with a wine-filled plastic bottle and packs of cigarettes hidden in their backpacks.

They sit on a dusty blanket, passing the bottle between them and watching the sunset. It's wonderful, for a while—they laugh and gossip and share cigarettes while coughing, but today, Kaja's heart's not really in it. Ever since she opened the newspaper and saw that headline a few weeks ago, something ugly coiled in the pit of her stomach, and she couldn't stop it, no matter how hard she tried. Suddenly, it was everywhere—discussed on the news, debated at family gatherings, whispered among the classroom tables. Who would've thought so many people were interested in supposedly preserving the sanctity of marriage?

"C'mon," her friend urges her, "what is it? You know you can tell me anything."

The sun's hanging low, casting long, slim shadows of the birch trees behind them. Kaja wasn't going to say anything at first—of course she wasn't—but lulled by the cheap wine and the impending covertness of the night, the words come sloshing out of her, and it feels good, letting it all out. She's never told anyone before, and although she feels lighter, she also suffers the uncomfortable waves of vulnerability wash over her.

She meets her friend's gaze slowly, skittish like a spooked animal would be, but is relieved in an instant—nothing appears to be changed. Her friend is smiling at her like she always does, and her hand comes to hold Kaja's in a gentle squeeze as if to say, *Don't worry, the world's still turning.* The warmth of her grasp is welcomed, as the chill of the dusk starts to settle. Except, now that Kaja looks more closely, did her friend always have those tinges of red in her brown eyes, or an unusual, sulfury smell to her perfume?

Suddenly, the grip of her hands becomes uncomfortably tight, and Kaja lets out a startled yelp. Tiny bones crunch like dry branches.

"You're hurting me," she whispers, dropping her gaze at their clenched hands, only to find her friend's fingers knotty and rotten. It's only then that she notices their shadows stretching out with the last ray of sunlight, one shriveled and feeble, and one horned and menacing, extending ominously into the dark grass.

She jerks her hand away in panic, scrambling to her feet, only to bump into someone. It's one of her high school classmates, the one with the bleach-fried hair and a perpetual stink eye, frowning at her with distaste.

"Would you watch it?" she snaps with an eye twitch and recoils away from Kaja as if the touch of their skin burned, joining the rest of the girls at the end of the locker room.

Ah. Locker room—that's where she is. That's swell. Kaja's standing there like a weirdo, crumpling her gym class attire with a rigid grip. Her fingers still buzz with pain, and she really wants to relax her hold, but for some reason, she just can't.

Hushed chatter and stifled laughter comes from the other side of the room. The girls are whispering with their hands around their mouths, stealing glances in her direction. Kaja doesn't need to know what they're talking about to feel shame strumming through her body, even though she knows she didn't do anything wrong. In fact, she barely did *anything*, except stand here quietly, clutching at her stupid sweatshirt.

Regardless, she still feels like she needs to hide, to swerve away from the others like they did from her, so she rushes over to the toilet stalls, careful not to look at anything other than the dusty tiles under her feet.

Once inside, Kaja sits down on the toilet seat. She finally lets go of the clothes; they fall on the dirty floor, but she doesn't care, because she's planning to skip class anyway when the coast is clear. This time, she won't even have to lie about imaginary headaches and painful period cramps.

I know it might not seem like it, but my fingers are broken, she'll say, because her fingers feel broken, even though they don't look broken. Who would've ever guessed that she'd end up a doctor? Certainly not her.

She waits and waits in the stall, but that cackling laughter is still coming from outside. The walls of the stinking cubicle are slowly closing in on her, and fuck, did the toilets always smell so bad?

Would you fucking hurry up and go do some fucking cartwheels in the gym?—she wants to yell out, but then something gurgles from the toilet, low and wet and slimy. Kaja lurches backward and watches the lid rattle before it flies open with a thud. Moments later, a horn peaks out of the toilet, and she runs out of the stall screaming, stumbling right into her aunt's kitchen.

Next to her, her cousin's staring at her, annoyed.

"What are you screaming about?" she demands, but all Kaja can do is stare a troubled stare while wheezing and sweating like a madman. "You're *so* weird," the cousin says before walking away.

Kaja collapses against the kitchen counter. Her nerves are running thin and she doesn't know how much of this she'll be able to take. She's parched from all the screaming, her mouth cottony and saliva thick and stringy. Rummaging through the cabinet for a glass, she hears her dad and her aunt talking on the terrace through a cracked window.

"So, does she have a boyfriend yet?" Kaja's aunt asks. "Mine is starting to get so boy crazy, I can barely keep up."

Dad murmurs something Kaja can't hear, and *oh*, that can't be good. He's usually a loud and cheerful man, only in the habit of murmuring when he speaks about things he deems uncomfortable.

Her aunt hums suspiciously. "Well," she says after a minute, "she certainly looks like the type."

Kaja almost drops her glass. Her dad murmurs again, and Kaja wishes he would just speak his goddamned mind. Also, she thinks that she doesn't look like the type at all, thank you very much. Don't they see that she keeps her hair nice and long, wears the same exact clothes as her classmates, and, most importantly, keeps her armpits shaved? Is everyone so oblivious to her efforts?

Her teeth grind in frustration. It's very Sisyphean, the way she keeps at it—she just can't seem to get it right, no matter how hard she tries.

Her throat clenches and her lips wobble pathetically, like a child's would. Resolved not to have a breakdown in her aunt's kitchen, Kaja takes a gulp of water to calm herself, but the lump in her throat only gets worse. Something is stuck in it, and she coughs and rasps until she feels thin strands dragging across her tongue. They're sharp and coarse, and she gags before spitting out a clump of black hair, but somehow there's always more and more and *more*, gushing out of her lungs. She sticks her hand inside, scrapes her tongue, claws her throat, but nothing helps—it's disgusting and vile, and she doesn't understand why things like these keep happening to her. She tries to be a good, normal girl, she swears, tries not to be so *weird*.

Kaja heaves and chokes, probably blue by now. Why is nobody helping her? She turns around, about to rush outside and scream, but instead of her aunt's dimly lit kitchen, she finds herself in a white, shiny room, so bright that she has to close her eyes for a second, wet clusters of hair momentarily forgotten.

She catches the familiar whiff of fresh laundry. Squinting, she realizes that she's standing in her office, back at Beautifully Beautiful, but the lights are a bit brighter, and the floor's all nice and shiny and polished, and it's furbished like something straight out of a fancy interior design magazine.

The urge to cough dies down. Her lungs still burn, but now that's just an afterthought, because there's a girl standing next to her, looking at herself in the mirror.

Her smile is beautiful and radiant, revealing a set of shiny, white teeth. The dimples on her cheeks compliment her bright beaming, and her lips are soft and plump, flawlessly symmetrical. Of course, she has the most darling button nose, small and blushing, just waiting to get booped—so adorable, so totally not weird at all. There are no pores or imperfections on her face, skin as smooth as a porcelain doll's.

A strand of long, maroon hair tucked away reveals a delicate and dainty ear, and Kaja doesn't need to see the other one to know it's equally as beautiful and seashell-like as this one. Dressed in a white, cinched dress, the girl resembles a Greek goddess, if Greek goddesses were sporting gravity-defying, perky boobs and tasteful BBLs.

In other words, she's perfectly crafted, down to every minuscule detail, and maybe that's why Kaja belatedly notices the *Bye-Bye, Babaroga* pamphlet clutched in her hands.

The perfect girl turns to her.

"Thank you, doctor," she says, "I love it," and it's all too good to be true.

Dumbstruck, Kaja slowly glances around the office, but nothing appears to be out of the ordinary—there's no horns peeking out behind the curtains, no ugly, crooked limbs tangled under her desk, waiting to slither their way out. Feral like a wild dog, she sniffs the air again, but it's clean and fresh, and Kaja's legs quiver in silent piety.

It worked, she realizes at that moment, and relief hits her like a ton of bricks, so hard she almost drops to her knees.

"You're very welcome," she barely manages to tell the girl, overcome with emotion, and the girl spins around with glee, dress swaying around her slender body.

Kaja feels light as a feather, lighter than she felt in years. It's pure bliss.

The girl swirls to the door, waving a slender hand at Kaja.

"Until we meet again," she sings, and Kaja only answers "Farewell," knowing that they won't, because that was the point of it all, wasn't it? The weight is lifted off her shoulders, that awful, heavy stone gone, and now Sisyphus is finally free, free to do anything he wishes for, without being called weird or disgusting or vile for just being himself.

A bottle of champagne is conveniently sitting on her desk. Kaja pops it open. Liquid gold drips down her fingers, but she doesn't care. She doesn't even need a glass, or a special toast.

"Jesus fucking Christ," is all she says before the bubbly liquid spills down her throat, deliciously smooth.

She chugs the whole bottle, just like that, champagne dripping down her chin. She wants more, so she looks around her beautiful office for another bottle. Who could deny her? It's a very special day, if not the most important day of Kaja's life. She'll do whatever she fucking wants to, thank you very much.

Except a sharp prick in her forehead brings her down from her high. She rubs a hand over her temples and says, "Absolutely not." The last thing she wants right now is a headache to ruin her celebration. But somebody's knocking at the door, and Kaja frowns, irritated, resolved to ignore whoever it is. It's probably Dejan coming for more, but she won't let him in this time, and she won't have trouble saying no to him, like she had in the past.

The knocking, however, doesn't stop—it's becoming louder and louder, pounding in the same rhythm as Kaja's burgeoning, stupid headache.

Agitated, she staggers to her feet and opens the door.

"No!" she yells, but it's not Dejan who's standing in front of her.

It's the girl, the beautiful, perfectly crafted—down to every minuscule detail—girl, but now her face is all wrong, ashen and contorted and sick. The beautiful white dress she wore is replaced by a dirty, crumpled scrub, torn in the middle. There's a huge hole in her stomach, blood and fat leaking out of it.

She still has that smile, though.

"A butcher butchers, Miss Broody" she happily tells Kaja, before she opens her mouth and shrills, blood gushing out of it.

Kaja shuts the door in her face and stumbles backward. Her foot slips on the polished floor and she ends up splayed against her back. The pain in her head worsens, creeps toward her eyes, her throat, her shoulders, and eyes. Tremors run through the whole of her body, the muscles spasming, convulsing, and stretching like a broken machine. Her skin itches, especially her forehead, and she rubs against it until her nails come out red, catching against something hard and ragged.

No, she thinks, and with the last of her strength she drags herself to the mirror, because it would be disgusting, *she* would be disgusting.

A bony, sharp mass is coming out of her forehead, tearing at the skin as it pushes its way through her skull. It's like a drill, and a drill drills, doesn't it? She hears the wet slaps of her peeled skin smacking against the floor. It's disgusting, *she's* disgusting, and it's not supposed to be like this, not anymore.

"You can't help it," Kaja says, her lips moving painfully against her will. The voice coming from her throat is distorted—it's not hers, of course it's not, but that rasp is horrifyingly familiar, and she knows better than to fight it.

In the mirror, her head tilts to the side.

"It's bound to come out eventually," her reflection tells her, lips curling in a bone-chilling smile, and all Kaja can do is scream and scream and scream—

—until she comes to with a wheeze, surrounded by the thick, black cover of the dark. Her hands comc to her forehead, groggy and heavy, but she only finds something wrinkled stuck against it.

"No horn," she mumbles. She wiggles and tries to get comfortable, but she can't seem to do so.

Something moves in the dark. Kaja's so sleepy she can barely keep her eyes open, and her head spins like a carousel. Two ember lights shine in the dark, blurred and fuzzy.

"God, can't you let me rest for one damned moment?" she wheezes, but it only comes out as a slurred groan. Pleading never worked before, though, so she waits patiently for the misery to start again. Except, now that she thinks about it, why is her mattress poking at her spine, all cold and bumpy?

Kaja frowns. It's so cold and drafty here, and it smells like earth, must and damp filling her lungs. It's only then that she notices the lack of hot, sweaty sheets that should cling to her body, and the soothing sound of Tihana's soft snores—Kaja's not in her bed, she's not even in the lodge, and where the fuck is she?

Panicked, Kaja clambers to her feet. Searing hot pain pulses in her head. The blurry lights are starting to take shape, and soon two hellish, red eyes are watching her sway on her feet.

This is new, and she doesn't like it. She's never been able to move before, and doesn't know how to play this game. Something has shifted, the rules have changed, and she knows she's not a fighter, so she staggers out of the cave and into the night, away from those red, glowing orbs.

***

It's still dark when Kaja waddles back to the lodge. Thankfully, everybody's fast asleep, and blessedly, nobody thought to keep the back door locked.

Hobbling her way through the living room, she catches a whiff of Butcher's burps still lingering in the air. Her stomach rouses, and while she tries her best to hold it in, she ends up throwing up on the threshold of Sandra's room. There goes their newly blossomed connection. *Oh*, Kaja thinks.

Once in the bathroom, she shrugs off the muddy boots and soiled clothes, shuddering violently as the unheated air pinches at her exposed skin. She sways on her feet, feeling another wave of nausea hitting her. Every once in a while little white sparks flash in front of her, reminding her that she somehow earned herself a textbook concussion. Did she fall? Or did she run into something headfirst? She can't seem to remember.

She must've run into that bitch Babaroga, she thinks, in that cave, and she smashed Kaja's head against a rock. *Yes, yes, that's what happened.* She remembers now. That wretched, stupid Babaroga.

Hesitantly, she finally glances at the mirror. There's dirt all over her—it's matted to her hair, splayed across her clothes and neck, yet somehow, her face has remained clean. She doesn't know what to think about that, so she doesn't. The sparks sparkle again, so she thinks about them instead.

There's also a kids' Band-Aid plastered across the center of her forehead—Hello Kitty, if she's not mistaken—but maybe she is, because she is so severely concussed. She slowly peels it off, winching with each pull on the skin, until an angry, red gash is revealed. It's fresh and pulsing, burning across her forehead.

For some reason, the cut itself seems relatively clean, but Kaja doesn't have an opinion on that, other than she's absolved of the tiring task of cleaning it herself. Whoever was responsible for it will receive her thanks later.

Another mystery is a thin, intricate braid plaited on the side of her head, falling gently over her cheek. Kaja's fingers skim across it, feeling the gentle ridges of the woven hair strands.

"Very pretty," she mutters, before she barfs again into the sink.

Her whole head throbs in pain and her likeness doubles in the mirror with every blink she takes. She's very tired and very confused, and it's very hard to think about anything other than the fact that she's very cold, so she turns on the water and watches it fill out the tub. She's not aware of her shaky hands coming to ghost over her forehead, as if expecting to find something other than a stinging wound.

"No horn," Kaja mutters to herself, climbing into the bathtub.

Hot water splashes around her, spilling onto the tiles. Kaja stays in the tub until her skin is red and raw and itchy, looking silently at the maroon water.

No horn, she wants to say, again and again, but the words die in her throat, suffocated by her soundless sobs.

Chapter 6

"THIS IS WHY I don't drink," Tihana muses, looking at the sorry state of them all.

They're in the living room, plopped around the coffee table. The reflection of the afternoon sun against its smooth glass surface is blinding Kaja's eyes, making her headache worse. The fact that she's sandwiched between Butcher and Dejan, when the mere thought of them makes bile rise in her throat, is also not helping. They're both manspreading like a couple of frogs on the couch, each with an IV sticking out of their arms.

"Thank *fuck* we're doctors," said Dejan as he stuck the needles in, while Butcher just grunted in appreciation. Robert only shook his head and watched them from the armchair. His constipated stare lingers on Kaja every minute or so, and Kaja senses that it might have something to do with Sandra's unfortunate drunk confessional. Dejan's also glancing at her with his dumb, smug smile, and Kaja wants nothing more than to sink into the couch and disappear, away from monster-ridden caves and icky pushy men and deadly medical negligence.

They were supposed to spend today in the woods, doing some 'fun bonding activities' (Sandra's words, not Kaja's, of course), but considering they didn't wake up until recently, those fun bonding activities were canceled. It's not like they couldn't entertain themselves in the lodge:

Kaja's defiled face charts are certainly proof enough. They're littered across the table, the floor, childishly ravaged with pens and markers. Mustaches, eyebrows, hairy moles, lasciviously pouty lips proclaiming lewd invitations, and of course, an obligatory dick or two. There's no question who the artists behind the doodles were.

A loud whirring noise comes from the kitchen. Robert's constipated stare intensifies. Maybe he's about to call off the rest of this wretched team building, Kaja hopes, and she can go and nurse her concussion in the privacy of her apartment, far away from those godforsaken hills and forests and caves, but his lips remain a solid, straight line.

Sandra's high-pitched cry comes a few moments later. "Kaja," she calls out, "would you be a darling and come help me?"

Kaja obeys, on her feet in an instant despite the general wooziness she's experiencing, thankful to get out of everybody's eyesight for a moment. Along with Robert, Tihana's also been eyeing her since she found Kaja this morning in their tub, babbling nonsense and splashing pink, dirty water out of the tub like a demented seal.

The experience wasn't pleasant for either of them.

She finds Sandra over at the kitchen counter, pouring some thick, mystery drink from a blender into a couple of glasses.

"Come, have some," Sandra says, ushering Kaja to sit on the barstool next to her. A barf-colored sludge is shoved into Kaja's hands. "Made by yours truly." Sandra winks. She suspiciously eyes the beanie that Kaja decided to pull over her forehead to hide the gash, but blessedly, doesn't comment.

With a shaky hand, Kaja lifts the glass and takes a sip. The smoothie feels like a thick, chunky goo, slithering its way slowly down her throat. She can taste something green, probably algae, spinach or something else that's green and deemed super healthy at the moment, but most of all she can taste the barf that she threw up yesterday. Her chest convulses.

"What a party last night, huh?" Sandra says, garnishing the drinks with pieces of parsley. Her tone is seemingly airly when she speaks, but with the way she's been tugging at that poor cluster of parsley, she looks anything but nonchalant.

"Hmm," Kaja agrees, trying not to gag.

"I might've been a bit sloshed, yesterday. Which is perfectly normal, right? We were all wasted, we were having fun, sharing a bit of gossip or two. And we do agree on that, right? That it's, like, *gossip*? Like, a totally fun and harmless chitchat between two loving, totally trusting colleagues?"

The smoothie sludge finally reaches Kaja's stomach. Though it's just some mushy, squashed fruit and veg, it sits uncomfortable in her gut, like she swallowed a bunch of rocks, and no matter how hard she tried to explain and rationalize to herself that they're not in fact there, or that she'll just shit them out, or that she'll even get them fucking ripped out of her, eventually, the rocks will drag her down—all the way down—and she'll end up glued to the ground, with nothing surrounding her but her useless, motionless limbs, and the dread of the own pained thoughts.

Back to square one. *God.*

The clink of the glasses brings her back from her trance.

Sandra's looking at her with a biting stare, gripping the tray tightly in her hands. "Best to forget those silly things I said, okay?" A beat passes before she adds, "And I'll forget that barf that mysteriously showed up in front of my door." Then she's out of the door, and Kaja spits the sludge back into her glass.

Gross.

***

It's a few hours later when Kaja finally reaches her breaking point.

She's sitting by the hot tub, skimming the bubbling water with her shaky hands. It's still and quiet outside—except for the sodden ground and leaves, there are no traces left of yesterday's downpour, but Kaja can't shrug off the feeling that another storm's just around the corner. The cocktail of painkillers has finally started working, though, and she can feel her mind clearing up a bit. There's a few things she's sure of: one—Butcher, Robert, Sandra, and Dejan are all covering up a murder, and are awful. There's not much to dwell on there. Two—she needs to quit, because this is really becoming a toxic (read: murderous) work environment. Three—there's a cave somewhere near this very lodge, where she's pretty sure she's encountered the very creature that has gleefully terrorized her since childhood.

Kaja sits there like a log, and doesn't know what to do with any of it.

Inside, Butcher and Dejan are running around, armed with a couple of tranquilizer rifles they dug up from the basement.

"Pew, pew!" they shout, ducking among the furniture. She imagines the darts flying out of the rifles, except they're not tranquilizer darts, they're real bullets that sting and prick and pierce through flesh, and they end up in their stupid, stupid heads.

"Pew, pew!" they shriek and giggle. They did some lines earlier.

They'll never get punished, Kaja thinks morosely.

Living with the fact that they'll all get away without it unscathed seems unbearable to her. And yet—and *yet*—she kept her mouth shut around Tihana, and her fingers didn't dial the police. Would she even be capable of doing either? Maybe she could just run, like she did last night out of that cave, and quit right here and now.

The glass door slides open. Robert steps out, puffing at a cigar, a glass of whiskey in his hand. He couldn't be more of a cliche even if he tried. He joins Kaja by the tub, sitting down uncomfortably close to her.

As usual, he doesn't beat around the bush. "Did Sandra talk to you?"

"Robert," Kaja starts, and hates the pathetic wobble in her voice, "I think I'd like to—"

"To what? Resign? Yap around? Go to the police?" He puffs at his cigar. "I wouldn't do that, if I were you. It's a well-established system, out there, and I'm still a wheel in that cog. Maybe a rusty one, admittedly, but still a wheel. And you, your idea, it's nothing but my oil." He puts out the cigarette on the edge of the tub, millimeters from her hand.

"I won't say anything," Kaja whispers, now beginning to feel claustrophobic even out here in the open, "just let me quit quietly and—"

But Robert cuts her off with a scoff. "You're so goddamn spoiled, you know that? You young people and your goddamn morals. You don't know how good you have it here. Do you want to go back to the ER and slaver away until you break? Or do you want to go to some stinking public clinic and treat coughs and hypochondriac grandmas all day long? Inspect smelly old men and screaming, snotty children? Do you, in fact, enjoy looking at swollen tonsils or ugly toenail fungus? Because that's what you're going to do if you back out of this."

Tears start to prickle in Kaja's eyes.

"Here's what you're going to do next. You'll keep your mouth shut and act as though Sandra's never breathed a word about Butcher around you. You'll get your sad little head out of your ass and pick out a candidate—a perfect candidate, because there's no room for mistakes here—and do the procedures, and you'll do all of it quickly. Time's money, and I love money." He lights up a new cigar and blows smoke up Kaja's face.

Are we clear? Robert's emotionless, botoxed stare asks her.

Crystal, her own echoes back.

***

"I think I'm going to stay for a bit longer," Kaja says. It's getting late, but the party's still in full swing (courtesy of the IV's and some coke).

Tihana's standing at the foot of the stairwell, face sour and squinting like she just sucked on some lemon. She leans in and stares Kaja up and down like a D-list movie detective. Kaja squirms, ignoring the painful throb in her sprained ankle.

"You're not going to do something stupid, are you?" Tihana whispers dubiously.

"Stupid, like what?"

"Stupid, like getting drunk and taking a walk through the forest. Again."

"Of course not," Kaja replies. "I'm just going to mingle for a while."

Tihana shoots her a look that says—*you, mingling?*—and Kaja can't fault her for that.

"Maybe I'm coming out of my shell," she offers weakly, praying that Tihana would back off and go to sleep. After a few moments, Tihana gives up.

"Uh huh," she hums, pursing her lips. "I just don't want you to see all tweaked and bloodied again when I wake up, alright?"

"Yes, of course."

"Promise?"

"I promise."

Kaja bids her goodnight and feels guilty as hell. Maybe that's what all big sisters do, she reasons; maybe they all lie and withhold dangerous, criminal information and run to the weird, potentially monster-harboring forest behind the younger one's back.

She still feels like thrash, though.

Once she hears the door close upstairs, Kaja carefully sneaks to the basement, and snatches a few tranquilizing darts. She also shoves a switchblade she found in the drawer into the pocket of her parka, just for good measure.

"What a killer party!" she hears Dejan yell as she slips out of the house, and heads back to the forest.

Chapter 7

THE GROUND IS SLIPPERY under Kaja's boots, mud and wet leaves sticking to their soles.

"It's going to be *sooo* fun," she mutters to herself, imitating Sandra's singsong voice and trying not to end up face-first in the grimy soil again. "Fucking idiot."

Her sprained ankle makes her wince with every step she takes, but Kaja pushes through the pain, determined to find the cave. She moves at a snail's pace, lighting the path with a shaky beam of her phone's flashlight.

The woods are eerily quiet and serene—Kaja's getting more and more uneasy as she progresses into the forest, the lodge diminishing to a tiny dot of muted light in the distance, until it's gone. The only sounds around her are the twigs rustling under her feet and her own labored breathing. The moon hangs high in the sky, casting a silvery light over the treetops. It would be kind of beautiful, if every crack of a branch didn't make Kaja shiver like a leaf. The path is progressively becoming more narrow, the weeds and bushes grazing her legs.

Kaja keeps her sight rigidly ahead. Occasionally, her eyes play tricks on her, finding long, bony figures hidden in the woodland, smiling wickedly behind the tree trunks. Every now and then, she swears she gets a whiff of the creature's stench. She looks down at the muddy path, shaking her head, pushing through her unease. The knife she brought feels like a lucky trinket, the weight of it radiating comfort. Every once in a while, her fingers find it in her pocket. The cool metal soothes her nerves.

Kaja's plan to just wing it and hobble into the forest, somehow finding the cave along the way, comes to an abrupt end as she emerges into the same clearing for the third time. By that point, she's been limping in the dark for an hour, trying not to get discouraged. Her determination wanes, however, as she takes stock of her current state: legs—shaky; ankle—pulsating with pain; head—throbbing and woozy. Her mental state—best not to be analyzed at the moment.

Frustrated, she plops into the dewy grass and coughs like a chimney-smoking grandpa, chest burning from the cold air she's been gulping.

"Ouch", she whines and wheezes. She's dizzy and tired, whimpering in the overgrown grass like a wounded animal. Her stomach growls and her mouth feels like sandpaper. The last thing she ingested was Sandra's mystery sludge hours ago. *God, that will be my last meal if this mission fails horribly*, she realizes with a pout. A bout of nausea clenches her stomach and she dry-heaves into the grass, feeling utterly miserable and pathetic.

The meadow is foggy and dark, flanked by the forest to the right and a tall ridge to the left. The wind rustles the trees, leaves floating across the clearing. Kaja wipes her mouth and stares at the seemingly endless forest spreading around her. Suddenly she feels so small and vulnerable, smaller than the ants crawling beneath her feet, and it's an unpleasant feeling, one that makes her turn off her flashlight, because she can't bear the thought of drawing any attention to her poor, minuscule self. It finally dawns on her—there's no way she could find the creature, if there even is one to be found.

She's baffled by her own foolishness. Was she really expecting to find a horned lady from her nightmares, a made-up folklore creature from a children's story, in some random forest in Kalnik? Waves of embarrassment flow through her, strong and sobering, sending her to her feet. She rubs her cheeks. What a merry chase her stupidity has taken her on.

She's about to limp back to the lodge when she hears a rustle across the meadow. The bushes crinkle and Kaja plops back into the tall grass with the speed of light. The wind stops its quiet murmur, leaving behind an unearthly silence.

The sudden stillness of the forest breaks goosebumps all over Kaja's spine. She once read somewhere that the woods only get deadly quiet when a predator is near. In her desperate search for Babaroga, she didn't even consider the bears or wild boars that roam this forest. Kaja holds her breath, panic rising through her chest, straining her upset stomach. She hopes she won't barf again, or get mauled by a wild boar.

After a few moments, someone emerges from the forest. They're tall and slender, cloaked in a black robe, almost indiscernible from the dark woodland. Kaja watches the figure move across the meadow, slow and smooth, almost like it's hovering above the cold ground.

That's no wild boar, she thinks dumbly.

It's dun and hazy, but Kaja can see a horn peeking under the hood, pale and white in the moonlight. It's like watching a silent film, the luminescence painting the scene in soft shades of gray, and although she's terrified, she can't help but feel a bit mesmerized at the sight. For a few moments, it feels like time has stopped, her mind reduced to smooth static.

Slowly, Babaroga glides across the clearing like an apparition, disappearing into the foot of the ridge with uncanny ease.

The wind starts blowing again, cold against Kaja's searing cheeks. She doesn't really believe in serendipity, but this feels close enough. She gets up to her feet, rubbing her chilled arms. It's not like more pleasant company awaits her back at the lodge.

Limping toward the ridge, she thinks about the outcome of her current predicament. Will she freeze, like in her nightmares, unable to move? Will the creature just snap her neck as she sets foot into the cave and put her out of her misery? Or is this all an elaborate and very lifelike hallucination, and she'll wake up back in Zagreb, in her sweaty, wrung sheets? She lets out a long sigh. All of the options sound bleak.

Kaja's legs quiver as she climbs up to the steep entrance of the cave. The mouth of it is narrow and well hidden, almost impossible to notice. There are no skulls thrown around its edges, no sinister script proclaiming *Do Not Enter* or *Babaroga's Hellish Cave* etched into the rocks. She can't help but to feel disappointed at the lack of theatrics.

"Well, here goes nothing," Kaja whispers and pushes through the crevice, floundering into the cave.

Darkness envelops her, thick and smothering. Before she can clumsily turn on the flashlight on her phone again, a faint scraping sound echoes through the cave. A few seconds later, a fire is burning at the far end of the cave, revealing a crouched figure next to it.

In the bright light of the flames, there's no denying the horn protruding out of the dark hood; it's pointy and bumpy and really fucking sharp looking, and an involuntary whimper escapes Kaja's lips. An earthy, humid smell fills out her nostrils, but Babaroga's stench doesn't seem to reach her yet. Kaja's heartbeat pulsates in her neck. Fear shakes her body like a leaf.

Slowly, the creature turns its head to the side. The hood slips from its head, and a pair of shiny, blood-ember eyes stare at Kaja, sharp and piercing. The wind is starting to get stronger in the background, filling the silence with ominous suspense. Kaja can't take it anymore.

"H-hello," she pushes out, for lack of a better introduction.

Babaroga just continues to stare in silence. Kaja shifts awkwardly on her feet, and well, oh. *Of course*—she kicks herself mentally—*she doesn't understand me*. How could she, when all that horned fiend can do is only hiss and growl and—

"It's you again," Babaroga says suddenly, and Kaja jumps, horrified. She talks? Her voice is low and gruff, echoing against the cave, leaving an eerie silence once it dies down. *Oh, god*, Kaja thinks and gulps nervously, gasping for air. Babaroga's never talked before. Is this some advanced rendition of her likeness, some hellish Babaroga 2.0 with a wicked tongue and the vocal ability to spend hours on end verbally berating Kaja?

Babaroga now regards her with interest, shifting slowly to her feet. Kaja takes an instinctive step backward. There's that awful feeling again, of being a tiny, helpless ant. Babaroga opens her mouth once more, and Kaja prepares herself for the wretched deprecation to start, for her weensy body to be crushed.

"How's your head?" is what Babaroga politely says instead, gesturing at Kaja's forehead.

Kaja must've misheard. "My head?" she repeats dumbly.

"Yes," Babaroga replies, "your head." She frowns, taking a measured step forward.

"You can talk," Kaja states, baffled. "With actual *words*."

"Hmm." Babaroga squints at her, taking in Kaja's ragged appearance and dumb-struck expression. "Maybe the head's not doing so well."

Unnerved, Kaja barks out a laugh, unable to stop herself. Out of all the possible scenarios she thought of, she didn't include *chitchatting with my years-long tormentor* on her list. The absurdity of the situation makes her lightheaded. She sways on her feet, hands coming to grip the harsh stone wall beside her. The jagged texture pokes at her palms, reminding her that *yes*, she's indeed in this cave, and *yes*, she's politely conversing with the actual Babaroga.

"Rest for a minute, if you want," Babaroga continues, retreating back to the fire. "I didn't clean your gash for you to bang into a rock again," she says with a snort.

Kaja finds this current predicament very strange. *Cleaned her gash?* The talking was a surprise, but this whole nursing her back to consciousness thing was even more surprising. Why go to all the trouble, if she's just going to bash Kaja's head in again? This Babaroga 2.0 really is perplexing. What a horned samaritan.

Curiosity hasn't pulled Kaja in for such a long time, she almost didn't recognize the feeling. Slowly, she walks over and sits on the damp soil. *I've come all this way* is how she reasons it. She wiggles her butt until she's comfortable and lets out a nervous cough.

"So, you came back," Babaroga states after a beat or two.

"Yeah," Kaja squawks, her mouth dry. She'd give about anything for a drink right now.

"Why did you?"

Kaja blinks. She's unprepared for the questions. Maybe hisses and scratches and sharp teeth sinking into her flesh weren't so awful after all, now that she has to talk. With actual *words*.

"Well, uh," she begins, trying to think of a plausible excuse when, almost godsend, a sharp sting pulls at her forehead. "I-I came back because I wanted to thank you for treating this," she lies and pulls at her beanie, revealing the gash.

"Oh," Babaroga says, looking at Kaja's bandaged forehead. "It was no trouble."

In the bright light of the fire, Kaja finally gets to have a proper look at the cloaked creature. She doesn't really resemble the creature that tormented her in her dreams—the long, goat-looking horn aside, of course. Her gaunt, heart-shaped face looks surprisingly youthful, with only a wrinkle or two. There's no cartoonish, saggy flaps of skin dragging her face downward, or centipedes crawling out under them: if she were a normal woman like her, Kaja reckons they'd most likely be the same age (and yes, she does consider herself a normal woman, definitely not a *weird* one, thank you very much).

Her skin is pale and pearl-like, almost translucent, with dark veins spreading delicately through her hands and neck, weaving a thunderlike embroidery that disappears into her worn-out, black cloak. Strands of thick, dark hair are tucked almost neatly behind her ears. Her nails appear to be on the long side, yes, but are no longer, or sharper, than Sandra's French-tipped manicure.

Most surprising of all, though, are the burgundy Doc Martens on her feet, and a pair of mismatched socks peeking out of them.

If Kaja didn't know better, she'd be thinking that she's looking at a Tumblr fashion icon back in 2012, or a high-couture fashion supermodel.

Huh, she thinks.

She glances around the cave next. It's not really as spacious as she imagined it yesterday, when she woke up smothered by the dark. The den is not much bigger than her one-bedroom apartment back in Zagreb, and even the atmosphere is eerily similar—there's a bunch of stuff piled in the corner: clothes, shoes, magazines, stuffed animals. Water bottles, snacks, and a plate or two—kind of like her own depression nest of laundry, miscellaneous junk, and chips wrappers. It's cold and drafty in here, just like it is back home with her old windows and expensive heating. Kaja has to admit that she finds the cave oddly familiar, and even a tiniest bit soothing.

Huh, she thinks again.

This whole ordeal is not really what Kaja imagined, and she suddenly feels terribly self-conscious. Was it rude to barge like that into someone's house—or stumble into a cave, if you want to be technical about it—uninvited, in the middle of the night? The least she can do is properly introduce herself, before the potential tormenting or attempted kidnapping starts. Maybe this well-mannered, 2.0 version is not so acquainted with her like the shrieking one that's usually taunting her.

"I'm Kaja," she blurts out.

Babaroga nods and tilts her head to the side again. "I would introduce myself, but you seem to know who I am," she says. "People usually run off screaming when our paths cross, if they've heard the stories."

"Yeah—" Kaja nods "—I-I've heard a thing or two." The fire's doing a lousy job of warming her up—shivers still run through her body, or maybe she's still, admittedly, the tiniest bit scared.

Babaroga frowns. She stands up, and a few seconds later, a warm blanket is draped gently around Kaja's shoulders. It smells of mildew, and surprisingly, some kind of perfume. Watching Babaroga rummage through the pile of things, Kaja wonders if a bottle of Chanel No. 5 will appear, but Babaroga only fishes out a teapot, a bottle of water, and a pack of cookies. Classic depression nest essentials.

With a smooth motion, Babaroga throws the cookies across the fire and Kaja clumsily catches them by reflex.

"Eat," Babaroga urges her. Kaja can't find a reason not to. Her stomach's growling by now, and the sugar might help her sharpen her senses. Not that she has much sense left.

"So, what do they say about me?" Babaroga asks calmly, her expression unreadable. "Is it the same old, same old?"

Kaja nearly chokes on a cookie. Some crumbles end up on the blanket, and she clumsily shakes them off. She coughs and wipes her face, hesitating. The blanket is starting to warm her up, and she wants to just pull it over her head and cocoon herself there in the dirt like a skulker.

Babaroga flicks her eyes from the water bottle she's been opening back to Kaja. She seems amused, like a flustered Kaja's some great sight to behold.

"You don't have to be shy," Babaroga says conversationally, opening the water bottle. "I want to hear it. It's been a while." She pours some water in the pot and holds it above the fire, patiently waiting for Kaja to start talking.

It takes Kaja a minute, but eventually, she does start to talk. In the nightmares she couldn't, so now, as she moves her lips and listens to the words form and leave her mouth, she finds it terribly freeing. *How refreshing*—she thinks as she rattles about.

She talks and talks, telling Babaroga about the children she likes to snatch and eat up, and then keep their tiny skulls as little trinkets. She tells her about the supposed broom that she uses to fly around, cackling in the moonlight. She divulges to her all about the sharp horn that she likes to poke and probe with, and how she smiles as her clawlike nails drag across soft skin. She informs Babaroga how she likes to creep on all fours against the ceiling, and how she just loves to sink her teeth into poor, innocent people, normal people who are not weird at all.

The water is boiling once Kaja's done. Out of all the times she could become a Chatty Cathy, now's a really bizarre one. She's a bit out of breath, and imagines that her cheeks are as searing as the kettle is. It felt good, to let it out of her system, but now that she finished the story, the glee which she felt while ranting about how awful the very creature sitting across her was fades rapidly. Babaroga listened to Kaja's story in relative silence, letting out only an occasional *hmm* and *is that so?* and *that's actually hilarious*. Her expression has been carefully neutral through the whole ordeal, revealing nothing about her current proclivities toward, let's say, violence and torture.

Kaja's starting to feel pretty bad. There she is, comfortably nestled into a warm blanket, cookies in hand, and about to receive a hot cup of tea. She looks over at Babaroga pleadingly, almost urging her to throw a dig at her—like, for example, pointing out Kaja's off-putting, fidgety behavior, or making fun of the belly pouch or her arm flab that she covers with baggy shirts and sweaters, but the insults never come.

What comes instead is a laugh—a simple, normal laugh, light and pleasant like the first whiff of spring air, or like, a very nice, fancy candle. It definitely isn't the weird, witchy cackling Kaja's used to hearing.

"People still like to fearmonger, don't they?" Babaroga says, the corners of her lips quirked upward. "How would it even be practical, to keep the children's skulls?" She rubs absently at her chin, reaching for the pile again. "It's getting much too crowded as it is here."

She pours the tea into a pink, polka-dotted cup. *Every day is a second chance* is written across it in a kitschy font. Their hands brush as she hands Kaja the tea.

How fucking quaint is this, is what Kaja's thinking at that moment. The sugar didn't help, apparently. She wonders if the painkiller cocktail she's been on is making her judgment all fuzzy and stupid. The cup is not really clean, and the bright, artificial-looking color of the tea doesn't seem appealing at all, but she still takes a sip. She's had worse things inside of her. Sandra's mystery sludge and Dejan come to mind.

"So, Kaja," Babaroga says, "what brings you to these woods?"

"A team building," Kaja answers on instinct, and then kicks herself internally. Less talking and more narcotizing would be great.

Babaroga frowns. "A team building?" she repeats slowly.

"What's a team building?" There's such a sincere, confused frown on her face, that Kaja can't help but crack a smile. Maybe being a horned hermit in the middle of the woods does have its advantages.

"It's a forced hangout among colleagues," Kaja explains, "meant to bring people closer together, build some morale."

"Has it worked?"

"God, no," Kaja says. "They're the worst."

"How so?"

Kaja laughs. Telling a monster about other monsters. The irony isn't lost on her. . She shakes her head and grips the teacup tighter. "They've all done some bad things. Like, pretty horrible things, you know? And yet, they think nothing can touch them, because, well, it can't. That's what's so fucking tragic about it—that's just how stuff like that goes, for people like them. And it's ironic, too, because we're doctors, you see, and we're meant to treat people, but they seem to do the exact opposite. It's hard to imagine, I suppose, how awful people can be."

There's something else at the tip of the tongue—the stupid treatment she devised—but she keeps that one quiet.

Outside, the wind has stopped its howling. The air thickens in the quiet it left in its wake. A branch pops in the fire, echoing across the cave.

"I can imagine," Babaroga mutters, dropping her gaze to the flames. The words Kaja spoke only a few days ago come back to her—*we don't even know who Babaroga really is, or how she came to be.* Who knows what this 2.0 version went through, to become what she is. A strange, primordial feeling runs through Kaja then, just like it did when she sat on that bench a few days ago.

"So you're a doctor," Babaroga states after a while, looking back at Kaja.

"Yes," Kaja replies. "A plastic surgeon." There she goes again, chatting away like she's on a freaking date.

"And what do plastic surgeons do?"

Kaja thinks for a moment. Nowadays, that's a really good question. "Well, it can be reconstructive surgery, meant to help people lead good quality lives, but our clinic doesn't specialize in that. What we do is purely cosmetic. You know, like lip fillers, botox, brow lifts, and such."

"To stop the aging," Babaroga says, and Kaja's eyebrows shoot up.

"Well, yeah," she confirms. "Or just generally, when someone's not really satisfied with the way they look, they can seek out a procedure to alter their appearance." She pauses for a moment. "I could probably help you, if you'd like."

"Help me with what?" Babaroga squints.

"Well, uh, with the..." Kaja trails off, clumsy gesturing toward her own forehead. Embarrassment flows through her instantly. She feels no better than Butcher and Dejan. In a way, she isn't, really, spewing unsolicited advice about women's bodies, and, in this particular case, forehead horns. What if Babaroga's perfectly satisfied with the goat-looking horn that's sticking out of her head? Maybe that will be the next trend: pointy forehead horns instead of brow lifts. *Well, she does carry it rather well*, she thinks, and she scolds herself. Maybe she's way more concussed than she thought she was. That would surely explain the warmth that's been pooling in her chest ever since she sat down.

"Ah," Babaroga says lightly, like they're not addressing the bony mass that's protruding from her head. "Is that why you're here? To alter my appearance?"

An uncomfortable tension seeps into the cave, and Kaja thinks, *touché*. Transparent as a pane of glass yet again.

"Well, no," she shoots out instead, not managing to keep a note of defensiveness out of her tone.

Babaroga shakes her head, the shadow of the horn dancing against the stone walls. "I don't doubt your medical skills, but I'm afraid they would be wasted on me. There is no cure for being the way I am."

"Well, would you let me examine you, at least?" Kaja presses. *This is not a social visit*, she needs to keep reminding herself.

"You're a strange woman, Kaja," Babaroga replies, not unkindly. "Why would you want to examine me?" She tilts her head to the side, regarding Kaja with a curious glance. The flames are curling in her irises, making them even shinier and more crimson in the dark of the cave. "There's nothing to examine. Not even a heartbeat."

"You don't have a heartbeat?" Kaja gawks.

There's a laugh again, but this time, a tinge of bitterness is laced through it. "Why would I have a heartbeat?" Babaroga retorts. "A beating heart is meant for humans, isn't it? Not a monster like me." Her gaze drops down to the fire. "People have tried to change me before," she continues quietly, staring into the flames. "I didn't quite appreciate that."

The admission leaves a somber silence between the two of them. Great. Now Kaja has to add compassion to the confusing mix of emotions she's feeling.

"I-I don't want to do that," Kaja assures her, but the words ring hollow and untrue even to her own ears. She squirms under her blanket. Didn't she come back here for that very reason? Weren't the darts in her pocket proof of that? She looks at Babaroga helplessly, trying to figure out if she needs to apologize, explain herself, or just smack Babaroga in the head with the teapot and drag her back to the lodge.

Babaroga lifts her gaze, and there's a horrifyingly familiar, broody frown on her face, making Kaja's heart give a painful lurch at the sight of it.

'So much potential,' Sandra would say. And sure, maybe she wasn't as wrinkled and monstrous as she was supposed to be, but still, she's the real deal. The horn is right there, pointy and sharp and full of bloodthirsty possibilities, illuminated by the muted light of the fire burning between them. Who could be more therapeutic than that? So what if she appears to be sentient, and surprisingly attentive, and—*oh, god*—even charming? For all Kaja knows, Babaroga's about to jump at her and claw at her face. Maybe she wants to lull Kaja in with her polite manners, warm tea, and delicious snacks, and then wring her neck like she would a chicken when she's least expecting it.

However, the switchblade and those damned darts remain untouched in her pocket.

Why are you here? she's asked, and well, wasn't that the question that's been on both of their minds ever since Kaja scurried into the cave?

"I told you," Kaja says, a cold clenching wringing her insides. "I came to say thank you."

Babaroga lets out a quiet huff. "Yes, so you've said," she presses, "but why are you really here?"

The uncomfortable silence that stretches out after is hard to bear. The words echo against the flame-lit walls, oppressing the air between them, pushing at their bodies, until it seems they're sitting miles apart. Kaja coughs again, fumbling with her empty teacup. Whatever's been circling between them seems to be gone.

Eventually, Babaroga shifts to her feet. "I think it's best for you to head back," she says. "Your colleagues might worry."

***

The walk back to the lodge is silent. Dark, murky fog has gathered around the path, making it look like a never-ending line. Kaja has no clue where they really are or how long they need to walk for, but she follows obediently after Babaroga, head bowed in penitence—she still feels awful about what she said back in the cave. And to think they were having such a lovely tête-à-tête. She tries to ease her guilt by reminding herself that just a few hours ago, Babaroga was a horned villain plaguing her life for years. Could Kaja really be blamed for her suspicion? Was she not allowed a moment of tactlessness without feeling like the worst person in the world? But still, Kaja sighs with regret, looking at the robe fluttering in front of her, wishing she could just reach out and find a way to express the whirlpool of emotion rising in her chest.

After a while, Babaroga stops abruptly, making Kaja bump gracelessly into her. A swift hand comes around her middle, steadying her.

"Your lodge is not far," Babaroga says, pointing ahead with her free arm. "Just follow the path and you'll arrive soon."

Kaja nods, shifting awkwardly on her feet. She can see the tiny dot of light through the fog. Going back seems absurd, but so does anything else. Babaroga's hand slips from Kaja's side, and she's feeling dizzy again, like an anchorless boat lost in the vastness of a murky ocean.

"Well, thank you again for everything," she manages to say. "For treating my wound, and for, uh, the tea and the snacks." Come to think of it, she doesn't remember the last time she was wined and dined like that. Dejan should take notes.

"It wasn't a hardship," Babaroga replies with a shake of her head. She regards Kaja with a look that's hard to pin down, and Kaja's suddenly really desperate to learn every microexpression that Babaroga has to offer. "Goodbye, Kaja," she says quietly, and then she's gone, the sound of her boots scraping against the ground.

Kaja stands there in the dark, staring dumbly at the figure disappearing into the fog. Her brow furrows. That's all?

Goodbye?

Goodbye?

After a few moments, her legs begin to move on their own accord, fast and resolved, like she's tethered by an invisible string. She barely even notices the pain in her ankle, with how angry she suddenly feels.

"Hey!" she shouts, and Babaroga turns around, surprised. Kaja takes a step forward, and points an accusatory finger toward her chest. "You told me you're a monster," she says, "and that you don't have a heartbeat, and *yes*, I can see that there's a goddamn horn sticking out of your forehead, but you've been nothing but lovely this whole evening, and I just—I don't understand."

Her breathing is getting winded again. She can feel her cheeks burning, feverishly hot against the cool autumn air. Her hand stills and hovers above the surface of Babaroga's cape, right where her heart should beat. She didn't even notice how close they were standing.

"What's inside, then, if not a beating heart?" Kaja demands. "You told me that I knew who you were, but I don't think I do after all, so please tell me, because I *need* to know." Her hands dig into the rough cloth of Babaroga's cape, her voice now quiet as the soft murmur of the forest around them. "Who are you?"

Babaroga stares silently down at her, eyes wide. She looks stricken and a bit lost, not at all the way a monster should look like. They're so close Kaja can see every little freckle on her cheeks, every delicate, thin capillary on her eyelids. Then, Babaroga smiles.

It's nothing like the smile in the cave, though. It's a sad, mournful smile, a smile so single-minded in its sorrow that it makes Kaja's heart skip a beat.

"Dear heart," she mutters quietly, looking into Kaja's eyes, and it's hard to tell in that moment, in those glowing, crimson reflections, where one ends and the other begins. "Do you honestly think it matters?"

Of course it does, Kaja wants to scream, but once again, her words fail her, so she shakily grabs Babaroga's face and pulls her even closer. Maybe, if she looks close enough, she'll solve this mystery, and things will finally start to make sense. The skin under her hands is soft and pliant, and Kaja swears she can feel Babaroga's breath across her cheek, but maybe it's just the wind that was playing cruel tricks on her.

Their noses bump. Kaja's ears are flaming.

"Of course it does," she manages to push out.

Something flies toward them, swift and soundless. Babaroga stumbles from their embrace, her hand reaching for the dart that's stuck in her neck.

A few moments later, Dejan and Butcher jump out of the bushes, rifles in their hands.

"PEW, PEW!" they shout.

Chapter 8

BABAROGA DROPS TO THE ground with an unceremonious thud. Kaja goes down with her, panicked, looking at Babaroga's eyelids fluttering before they shut.

Heavy, cumbersome steps approach them.

"My, my!" Butcher crouches beside Kaja, his eyes wide as marbles. "It looks like we really did catch something, after all." After a few moments, Dejan creeps closer, mouth hanging wide open.

"Kaja," Dejan whispers, nudging at Babaroga's side with his foot. "What the *fuck* is that?" He sniffs and wipes at his nose. There's still specks of white stuck there.

Kaja opens and closes her mouth helplessly. *My nightmare*, she wants to say, but only whimpers pathetically. An owl hoots in the distance, filling the silence.

"It looks so real," Butcher contemplates, eyeing the horn with his bloodshot eyes. "How the hell did you manage to do this?"

Kaja shifts on her feet, silent dread spreading through her body. *It's just a figment*, she wants to say, *it'll go away once the sun comes up*, but that's not right, is it? Ever since she set foot in this fucking forest, the lines of reality started to blur. What a literal nightmare this is.

"I found her," she says dumbly, "in the forest." The guys burst out laughing, their guffaws echoing in the forest.

"Yeah, whatever you say, doctor Frankenstein," Dejan tells her, scrubbing his glassy eyes.

"I-I didn't do it," she repeats, louder. "I told you, I just found her." But neither Dejan nor Butcher seem particularly convinced.

"Well, whatever that thing is, let's get it back to the house. I bet Robert will find it interesting." Gracelessly, Butcher picks Babaroga up, her body lax in his hands. "Let's get this show on the road."

Please, let's not, Kaja thinks, but once again, her legs seem to have a mind of their own, and she ends up following the guys down the path. Each step is like a punch to her gut, bashing her very fragile, very squishy core. She really was on the cusp of something, earlier—what that exactly was, she doesn't know. But it was *something*, she feels, something important, and now it's gone.

The guys' chatter fades into background noise, and for a moment, Kaja feels like she's nowhere, stuck in a cage of her own making. She looks at Babaroga slung across Butcher's shoulders. It does something weird to her heart. It feels like it's made of glass, all frail and dainty, and just one misstep will shatter it and the sharp little shards will pierce her lungs.

Babaroga's head sways sluggishly with every heavy step Butcher takes—Kaja's watching it swing side to side until the nausea in her stomach becomes overpowering. She keeps her eyes on the ground for the rest of the walk.

Every now and then, her hands find the darts and knife in her pockets, but they don't linger around them much. Even if she were to pull them out, she wouldn't know who to swing at.

***

"Special delivery!" shouts Butcher as they arrive back to the lodge. They walk through the hallway and into the living room like a bunch of joyful scouts coming back from their expedition. Kaja wants to scream.

Butcher dumps Babaroga on the table, wine glasses and ashtrays flying to the floor. The loud crash of the glass breaking doesn't stir Babaroga—her eyes are still closed, one arm loosely hanging from the edge of the table. The words she spoke linger in Kaja's mind, dark and permanent like spilled ink.

Is that why you're here? To alter my appearance?

If a knife got buried in her neck, would she even bleed? Kaja's embarrassed that, despite her medical background, the logistics of the operation—or the killing, whatever—haven't really crossed her mind. According to Babaroga, there's no heart beating inside her chest, no blood pumping through her veins. She is a monster, a tale, and how is Kaja supposed to kill something that won't bleed?

Except, the tranquilizer *did* work, and that must mean something, there must be some dots to connect, a lesson to learn, and fuck, Kaja's always been shit at actually dealing with stuff.

Behind her, Butcher sighs. "She's pretty heavy for a sack of bones and dried skin," he huffs, massaging his shoulder. He retrieves a can of beer from the fridge and guzzles it down, before letting out his signature burp.

"You know, I thought she'd be uglier, to be honest." Dejan sounds a bit disappointed. "Like, she doesn't even look that old." He takes a fork and slowly pokes at Babaroga's lips. Kaja's stomach convulses as he probes at Babaroga's gums. "Even her teeth are pretty good," he concludes petulantly.

Kaja's on the verge of tears. It's all so backward. This was supposed to be her project, her escape, and now Babaroga's lying on the table, exposed and helpless, on display for everyone to ogle at.

As on cue, the back door slides open. Robert and Sandra parade inside, wet and drunk. Robert's neck is covered in smears of pink lipstick and Sandra's adjusting her shiny, golden bikini.

"Oh, you should all get into the hot tub. It's absolutely *divine*!" she boasts, fumbling with her top's straps.

Beside her, Robert freezes. "Jesus," he proclaims, staring at the unconscious horned creature casually lounging in their living room. His eyebrows jump almost all the way to his hairline, fighting for dear life against the layers of botox. "What is this?"

"It's our candidate!" Dejan says smugly. "Miss Babaroga herself." He walks up to Kaja, pulling her close. "She's really made an effort, huh?" A messy kiss lands on her cheek, and Kaja thinks she'll throw up in her mouth. Just as she wiggles her way out of his embrace, Sandra runs up to her. Her stilettos clink against the floor.

"I told you," Sandra cries out, grasping Kaja's shoulders with an iron grip. "I *told* you you could do anything!" She leans in, eyes narrowing in suspicion. "Was it manifestation?" she whispers. "You *have* to credit me."

"N-no," Kaja replies, "I found her in the forest. I didn't—"

"Well, you certainly did something to trigger...*this*," Robert cuts her off, waving a hand in Babaroga's direction. "She most certainly didn't become so...unnatural without any intervention, right?"

Kaja's eyes are stinging. She takes a deep breath as she feels another wave of dread wash over her. It's like she's never left her childhood bedroom.

"I didn't do anything," she repeats, throat clenching painfully around each word. Tears prickle at her eyes, and she rubs them raw with the sleeve of her jacket. Wasn't this what she wanted? A perfect candidate—*the* candidate—is lying right in front of her, weak and defenseless. It's the chance she's been waiting for for years, but now, Kaja feels like a kid caught red-handed, guilt and shame and fucking *indecisiveness* washing all over her. "I didn't do it," she whispers, but nobody is listening to her—they're too busy gawking at the horned woman lying in front of them, rubbing their hands together like they've just won the biggest prize in the world.

"Exquisite," Robert says, circling the table like a cat. He huffs, shaking his head in disbelief. "This is perfect. *She* is perfect. I'm mean, obviously, she's fucking hideous, with that horn sticking out of her, but that's what we're here for, right?" His eyes turn to Kaja, pinning her down with an impish gaze. "We'll make her right, won't we?"

A tear falls down Kaja's cheek.

"Ah, tears of joy!" she hears Sandra screech. "Let's make a toast, once we dry ourselves up. We've got a bottle upstairs." She pulls at Robert and they both head up, giddy and euphoric like a couple of drunk teenagers. Dejan's right behind them, muttering something about "needing more blow."

It's finally quiet downstairs. The night outside is still dark and dreary, even though the clock ticking away on the wall shows it's almost dawn. To Kaja, sunrise seems eons away. She wants to shake Babaroga's shoulders, and for the woman to open her eyes again.

And yet, she remains stiff and useless, standing there like a statue.

This is what you've been waiting for, the voice in her head reminds her. It's like she's back to being the little girl she once was, scared out of her mind, desperately trying to make sense of the apparition that's stuck to her. Kaja shoves her hand down her pocket and grips the switchblade. She tried to be a good girl, she really did—she tried to blend in, tried not to be so fucking weird. This may be her only chance.

Babaroga's right there, vulnerable and unmoving: it's strange to think that their roles are finally reversed. Kaja tightens the grip around the handle.

People have tried to change me before, Babaroga told her. *I didn't quite appreciate that.*

The metal blade is cold and smooth against the skin of her palm. Despite the cool breeze flowing through the open door, a bead of sweat drips down her neck. Her insides coil like a pit of snakes.

Butcher's right behind, towering against her as giant and solid as a brick wall. His fetid breath scorches her ear. Foul, foul, *foul.*

"She's going to be a wonderful doll, once we're through with her," he mutters. "I can't wait to cut into her."

With a swift motion, Kaja slips the switchblade from her pocket and flips it open. It's buried in his neck a second later, sliding in with a surprising ease.

A wet gurgle escapes Butcher's throat. Blood lands on Kaja's face, squirting like a spray of ketchup from Butcher's meaty neck. Gross. She pulls out the knife as quickly as she plunged it in, and then, more blood spurts out, covering both of them in red. Butcher stumbles backward and squeals like a pig before he sinks to the floor.

A flood of bubbly blood gushes out of his o-shaped mouth. He's about to burp his last burp.

Kaja watches him squirm on the floor, heaving for air, until, eventually, his jerky twitches stop.

Butcher butchered, Miss Broody, is all she has time to think, before clumsy footsteps thud down the staircase.

"Butcher!" Dejan shouts. "Where the hell did we put the rest of the fucking—"

His mouth snaps shut once he stumbles into the room. "What the fuck?!" he screams. The rapidly expanding pool of blood grazes his shoes, making him gag. "What happened?" he chokes out, covering his mouth with his sleeve.

"I stabbed him," Kaja replies by reflex. She thought it was fairly obvious, as she's still gripping the switchblade. To better paint the picture, she even lifts the knife.

"What the fuck, Kaja?!" Dejan yells, watching Kaja carefully step over the blood and stand next to Babaroga.

"I'm taking her with me," Kaja says, strangely calm. Her hand finds the rough fabric of Babaroga's cape. Dejan gapes at her.

"What? No way!" he wails. "This is our golden goose." He walks over to Kaja, shoes wading through the puddles of blood. His pupils are two dilated saucers. "Look, we can bolt, okay?" he whispers desperately, grabbing Kaja's arm. "Let's take her and ditch the others. Fuck them. We can do the treatments ourselves."

Kaja shakes her head. "No," she says, shrugging out of his hold.

"No?"

"No, Dejan, I will not come with you." Sandra would be proud of her newly found assertiveness.

He scoffs. "Why the hell not?"

Under all that blood, the cheeks of Kaja's face flush. She clears her throat. "I uh, I may have finally sorted out my priorities," she says bashfully, like she didn't just stab someone in the neck minutes ago. Her grip against the sleeve of Babaroga's cape unconsciously tightens.

There's a beat of silence, before Dejan's eyes widen in realization. "No way!" he shouts. "You're choosing a fucking monster over me?" He thumps at his chest maniacally like a gorilla. "A *girl* monster? Over *me*?!" he wails, and well, there's nothing like a man's broken ego. He twists at Kaja's wrist and the switchblade clatters against the floor.

Shit, Kaja thinks, before she's being shoved against the nearest wall, her wrists pinned above her.

"I knew you were fucked up, but I never thought you were *this* fucked up!" Dejan spits out. Specks of saliva land all over her face. "You've missed the opportunity of your lifetime! We could've been so good together," he snarls, "but this, this is something even my dad can't cover up." One of his hands finds Kaja's throat. "You can't just go around killing people!"

"And he can?" Kaja pushes out, eyes dropping to Butcher's lifeless body on the floor.

"O, cry me a river! It was a mistake!" Dejan shouts in her face. "You ungrateful bitch," he bites out, tightening his fingers against her neck. "Always so fucking self-righteous, huh?"

Kaja tries to wiggle out of his hold. If only Tihana's imaginary Krav Maga boyfriend were here. He'd know what to do. Her vision narrows down—it's not fair, she thinks, that the walls of the room are closing in on her again, when she finally sort of figured it out.

"Fuck you," she wheezes, "and your fucking dad."

The choke hold is unrelenting. The room spins and her ears buzz. Her eyelids become heavy and lax. Through the dim haze that's beginning to veil over her, Kaja thinks it a shame that she'll never know who Babaroga really is, or why she followed Kaja around all of those years. The lack of oxygen is making her weepy and sentimental, but maybe it's also something else. Her body trashes and convulses, until her vision goes dark.

Then the pressure around her neck suddenly disappears, and she heaves like a newborn baby.

The strain on her lungs is painful. She heaves and heaves, until her vision slowly comes back into focus. Dejan's wide eyes are the first thing she sees. They're looking downward, twitching. Kaja follows his gaze.

The second thing she sees is the tip of a goat-looking horn peeking out of his stomach, sharp and blood slick.

"F-fuck," Dejan pants out, before the horn pulls out in a swift, brutal motion. He stumbles back, dropping to the floor. Kaja's legs give out next. She lets herself slide down against the wall and watches as Babaroga follows a wailing Dejan across the room. Her step is so sure and steady, the flutter of her robe trailing behind her.

"Very pretty," Kaja murmurs.

Eventually, Dejan trips because, of course, it's very hard to walk with a huge hole in one's stomach. He's sobbing and whimpering on the floor, calling out to his dad for help. Idiot. His expensive, beige cashmere sweater is drenched with blood, and a bit of viscera here or there. It's hard to tell what's what, with the way he crawls on the floor like a slug, wiggling his way through the pools of Butcher's blood. The whole room reeks of copper and sweat and sheer havoc.

"You fucking monsters," he cries, clumsily catching a handful of his entrails that just keep sliding out, "you foul, fucking lesb—"

He doesn't get much further. Thank god the boots are red, and not white, because cleaning them would be a nightmare. The bone crunching is gross, sure, but with every stomp of Babaroga's red Docs against Dejan's head, Kaja finds it easier to breathe.

Once there's nothing but mush under her soles, Babaroga stops. Her eyes flick back to Kaja, before they drop down to the glass table between them. Kaja's heart clutches violently in her chest. She forgot the face charts that were splayed against its surface.

Once again, Kaja can't read the expression which Babaroga stares her down with.

Kaja opens her mouth. "I'm sorry," she's about to say, but the sound of Sandra's pointed heels snaps both their heads toward the stairwell.

"What's all the commotion about?" Sandra singsongs, holding a bottle of champagne in her hands. "Don't start the celebration without us! I'm already planning the—"

She finally lifts her head and stops, taking in the scene in front of her. The shriek of horror comes a few seconds later, and well, Kaja can't really blame her: between Butcher lying marinating in his blood, Dejan's bashed-in brains splattered on the floor, and a freshly awoken, red-horned Babaroga, Kaja would probably be a bit fazed herself. Then Robert's there too, yelling and slipping on blood.

The four of them are soon on the floor, wrestling for dear life. It's brutal and inelegant, and they're drenched in Butcher's blood and Dejan's brain. Sandra accidentally smacks Robert across the head with the champagne bottle.

Kaja claws at Robert's face, swearing she can feel the botox moving under her nails. Robert punches Kaja in the ribs in return, and Babaroga kicks Robert's balls with her nasty boot. He howls like a wounded animal. They slip and slide on the slick floor. Someone's puked along the way, and it stunk up the place even more.

Eventually, they split. Robert's hauled Kaja to feet, holding her in a choke hold, while Babaroga and Sandra have ended up outside, dragging each other by the hair and screeching like a couple of banshees.

"I disappeared a brat like you once, and I can do it again," Robert whispers into Kaja's ear. She rolls her eyes, for once thankful she doesn't have to hold the urge in anymore. She's so fed up with old men telling her what they'll do, with their stinky breath parching her cheeks.

Kaja's hand slips into her jacket. She grabs the dart from her pocket and blindly pokes behind her back with all of her strength, hoping for a lucky hit. A pained yelp informs her she's been successful.

Free from the hold, she turns around to see Robert desperately fumbling to get the dart out of his eye. Behind him, the glass table reflects his jerky motions. One-eyed and understandably perturbed, he doesn't even see Kaja's hands coming.

The shiny surface breaks under his weight. He sinks until he's nestled among the shards of sharp, broken glass. His efforts to move only slide the fragments deeper into his skin, slicing his arms, his face, his neck. The constipated stare on his face warps into a twisted grimace of pain and disbelief.

Kaja hovers above him, looking at his bloodied face. She waits for a twitch, or for some botox to gush out of his cut-up face, but he remains perfectly still. His eyes wide and dull, staring at the ceiling, and her question answers itself.

Are we clear?

"Crystal," she concludes and heads out to the backyard. Her mind's crossing tally marks. She sighs and cracks her knuckles. One more to go.

Sandra and Babaroga are splashing around in the hot tub. It's looking like Sandra's got the upper hand, pushing Babaroga's head underwater.

Kaja hobbles to the hot tub. "Sandra," she says.

Sandra lifts her head, and they stare at each other for a moment. Then Kaja raises her hand and punches Sandra in the nose as hard as she can. There's an awful crunching sound and they both shriek. Blood splashes down Sandra's nose and Kaja cradles her hand with a whine. It looks way easier in the movies.

Quickly, she reaches for Babaroga—her skin's cold and clammy under Kaja's fingers. She's heaving like crazy, and with the way her limbs go supple and pliable, she's hard to grasp, but somehow, Kaja pulls her out of the tub.

"Go," she tells her, before Sandra grabs at her jacket.

Water splashes around them while Sandra's throwing punches like a madwoman. The tub still produces swirling foam beneath them, stirring the water with sparkling bubbles. It ramps up the dramatics even more.

"You fucking maniac!" Sandra screams. "I *knew* something was wrong with you!" Her long nails claw at Kaja's face, scraping down every inch of available skin. For a while, it's a desperate catfight. Every once in a while, when they stop to catch a breath, the name-calling starts. "You deranged, fugly weirdo!" Sandra howls; "You desperate, nasty gold-digger!" Kaja shouts back, and they go on like this for a while. Kaja believes that it's quite therapeutic for the both of them.

Finally, after a lucky, well-landed blow to Sandra's left boob, Kaja manages to grab her by the hair. She pulls out a handful of extensions, making Sandra look at her incredulously.

"You bitch!" she shrieks, tufts of short, wet hair sticking out of her head. "Do you know how much they cost?!"

"No," Kaja breathes, and uses the last ounce of strength left in her body to shove Sandra's head underwater.

It takes longer than she expected. Unlike Kaja's 'raw and unpolished attitude', Sandra's squirming body needed a *big* push. Fuck. Her arms are burning, but she doesn't let go. The wind blows again, cold against her soaked body.

After a while, the splashing finally stops. The water stills, circles calmly spreading toward the edges. Kaja slowly lets go of Sandra's head and it plops back to the surface like a plastic ball. The bleach-blond extensions float almost peacefully around her. A strand is still wrapped around Kaja's fingers, and she shakes it off with distaste.

A warm weight comes to sit on her shoulder. *There goes nothing*, she thinks again. She turns around.

Babaroga's staring at the floating body with an awestruck look on her face, like drowning someone was the most romantic gesture someone could do for her. Kaja lets out a long breath. Maybe she's starting to get her expressions after all. A pair of hands wraps around her waist, and soon she's out of the tub, clumsily stumbling forward.

Tension seeps out of her body. Sluggish and lax, Kaja melts into Babaroga's embrace, head nestled in the crook of her neck. The treetops rustle gently in the crisp breeze, surrounding them with a soft murmur.

They stand like that for a while, covered in blood and guts and sweat. Kaja's breathing finally slows down—somehow, she even feels at peace, like she did in that dream-conjured office. Who would've thought she just needed to commit multiple degrees of murder? Nothing's left of her doubts, her scruples. There's a warm buzzing spreading through her chest instead, and a bit of grief clutches at her heart when she thinks of all the years she spent running away from it all.

Kaja noses the silken skin of Babaroga's neck—she still smells like the cave, and a bit of copper and sweat. Her lips graze the skin above the jugular. Kaja smiles before she lifts her gaze.

There's a gash on Babaroga's cheek, red and shiny, and Kaja's going to return the favor later, but now, there are more pressing matters at hand. She tucks a strand of damp hair that clung to Babaroga's rosy cheek behind her ear.

I can't believe I wanted to change you, Kaja thinks, before she finally leans in.

Babaroga tastes like earth and iron, and something sweet, something new Kaja cannot name yet; something alive and trembling, finally in her grasp, and they don't stop, not until they're both gasping for air.

The fog's clearing up, lingering around the ground. A few birds fly above them, disappearing into the forest. Their chirping lingers in the air, bright and telling: there's a sunset hiding behind the hills. It'll rise soon, and it's going to be warm and beautiful. The first rays of sunshine are almost here, piercing through the mass of the dawn-lit sky. Kaja can feel it coming. She laughs, and soon, Babaroga joins her, and they both laugh and laugh and *laugh*, giddy in their embrace, until a shriek pierces through it.

Shit, Kaja thinks. *She really did sleep through it.*

"You promised!" Tihana wails, standing by the glass door.

Kaja looks at her bloody, viscera-covered body. She did end up getting all bloody despite her word. "Uh," she says. "Sorry."

But as Kaja stands there, Babaroga's hand warm and solid against hers, she isn't, in fact, sorry at all.

PART II:
THE MONSTER

Chapter 0

I COULDN'T TELL YOU the exact date, nor the year I was born. Time's a fickle, silly thing when you're someone like me. I do, however, remember the village I grew up in pretty well, so maybe I should start there.

It was a small village in northern Zagorje, resting at the foot of the surrounding hills, with a quick, glistening stream between them. Before I was born a second time, I never really ventured past the stream and up the hills, but now I know every inch of the woods that spread through them, each weed and oak tree that spurted from their soil.

The village was a plexus of wide, dusty paths, beaten down by many feet over the years into distinctive paths. Small, wooden houses were settled along them like hand-carved trinkets. In the heart of the village lay a small square, with a modest church gracing the far end of it. It was a quaint, nice village, not unlike any of the others at that time. Fields of maize surrounded it, shiny and golden in the sun if the year was good. I loved to rummage in the maize, as all kids did. We spent the summers running through the fields, playing hide and seek under the scorching sun, limbs full of cuts from the sharp leaves that stuck out of the stems.

For all our hardships, we fared well—the villagers were a hardworking, tight-knit community, with their health sturdy and stomachs relatively full.

Everyone contributed something: cow's milk or cheese, knitted, warm bedspreads and covers for the harsh winter, or even a nice word or two. Although I was restless by nature, I was happy to live there, and rarely thought about leaving. For most of my life, I reckoned I would die there, buried in the graveyard on the outskirts of the village, next to the people I loved the most.

I don't remember who said this—maybe it's just one of those wise, contemplative truisms people tend to repeat with a mournful voice—but someone once told me that you can't choose the way you die, but you can choose the way you live. Those words stuck with me, and I often thought about them. I have tried my best to live by them, but in the end, it appeared I couldn't choose either of the two.

***

The first time I was born, it was early spring.

Spring was a lot colder in those days, and the snow outside hadn't even started melting yet. I didn't, however, feel any cold upon my arrival: the world I was welcomed into seemed warm and kind. There was always something to keep me warm—my grandfather's knitted cape gently wrapped around my shoulders, the smoldering fireplace or the steaming cup of tea my mother made me.

Most of my early childhood was spent in the company of my mother and grandfather, and a bit later, Jaroslav and Agata. My mother was a harsh woman; words were never her strength, leaving me to wonder where I got my love and talent for yapping about.

So I sought out my grandfather most of the time and talked his ear off while he worked on the loom.

He was very gifted at weaving, making wonderful, warm covers and beautiful capes, and I soon fell in love with the trade.

"At least she won't get in any trouble if she's glued to the loom," I overheard my mother say to a neighbor once. By that time, I'd already started making a reputation for myself as the local rascal, wandering through the village at night and knocking on our neighbors' windows, or letting out farts during Mass. That one was a classic in my repertoire.

"All the pushing and tearing I had to endure to bring you into this world, and this is how you repay me?" my mother would fume.

My grandfather was the only one who understood my rebellious character.

"There's not a thing I would change about you, dear heart," he told me before he passed away. Resolved to listen to his advice, I never did change—that is, not until the choice was made for me.

***

The first time I saw the twins, they were hiding behind their mother who came to pick up the bed covers my grandfather made. Those were one of the last spreads he made, and I took no pleasure in giving them away. My grudge went away quickly as I saw two mops of ginger hair peeking toward me, shy and wide-eyed.

I stared right back, unabashed. We were about the same age, limbs gangly and cheeks ruddy, like most children here were. I've never, however, seen a set of twins before, and I remember looking at them, awestruck, thinking, *these are going to be my best friends in the whole wide world.*

Luckily, my admiration wasn't one-sided. The next morning, I jaunted around the village until I found them jumping ropes on a dusty path, soot rising with every hop they made.

"Can I join?" I asked, and the twins looked at each other in silence.

"I'm Jaroslav, and this is Agata," the boy said eventually, and handed me the other side of the rope. The three of us didn't part since, not until it became inevitable.

***

It was Easter. The Mass was very boring, and it stretched out even longer than usual. However, I was very excited, squirming on the uncomfortable wooden bench next to my mother, stealing glances in Jaroslav and Agata's direction every now and then.

The priest was reading some passage from the Bible. Something about Jesus being reborn, rising from the dead. I didn't think much of it. Being reborn? Rising from the *dead*? I just huffed under my breath, much to my mother's dismay. I was more interested in the things that could be held and grasped, like the firm bed covers or cloaks I weaved on my loom, or a nice, warm loaf of fresh bread laid out for breakfast. To me, the knicks and knacks of God-praising sounded pompous and made-up, the countless rules and kneeling and damn *obedience* getting on my nerves.

The thuribles swung, stinking up the place with a pungent, herby tang. It always made me a bit queasy, that smell. Feeling a bit dizzy, I focused my eyes on the priest, wishing he would pick up that damn chalice already.

A tall and imposing man, his voice a deep and raspy baritone, he was propped up behind the altar like a statue draped in white cloth. Unlike the squeaky inflection of our former priest, his chanting echoed against the walls of our small church, reminding me of the roar of thunder before a summer storm.

I bowed my head as my mother hissed at me to *for the love of God, stop fidgeting already*. My hands ended up in my lap, laid at the top of my knees. My apron hid the relief of the grains of corn still stamped into my skin. Even after a week, it still itched and burned, the skin red and aggravated to the touch. The priest punished the twins and me yet again last week, making us kneel on the corn for hours for talking during Mass.

I took a glance at him again. Dumb, awful priest. Many rumors were whispered as he came to our village about a year ago. Due to his years of traveling through different countries, he was considered to be peculiar and eccentric. He rarely smiled, and generated an aura of graveness around him. It took a while for the villagers to warm up to him, the way he loomed around the square in his long, black robe. *If he weren't God's man, he'd be the Devil's*, one of our neighbors said, and while I didn't regard religion in a serious manner at all, I couldn't deny the shivers that ran down my spine when he pinned me down with his deep scowl.

He did, eventually, become a well-liked figure in the community, being one of the few educated and literate people in the village. Though he was strict and had a love of rebuking, his direct and practical nature made him often sought for advice. Jaroslav and Agata's parents were especially fond of him, and would often invite him for tea at their house, much to the twins' dismay.

My fingers played with a loose thread in my skirt. The hem of it was still damp, and it filled me with glee and anticipation I barely managed to hide.

My mouth quirked up as I saw the priest reach for the chalice of wine. This was the moment I'd been waiting for since the twins and I parted ways and rejoined our families before Mass started.

Seeking retaliation for our bruised knees, Jaroslav and I had snuck into the sacristy, Agata keeping guard outside the door. Jaroslav had been pacing up and down the narrow room, looking nervously at the portraits of saints hung up on the wooden walls.

"Maybe we shouldn't," he'd whispered, standing in front of the jug of sacramental wine on the table. "What if he figures out it's mine?"

I'd huffed, unimpressed. "How would he know it's yours?"

Jaroslav had only shrugged and chewed at his fingernails. I loved the twins with all of my heart—how could I not, even after all that happened—but sometimes, his and Agata's timid nature irritated me to no end.

"Well, if you're not going to do it, I will." I'd pushed him out of the way and grabbed the jug, then hoisted my skirt up.

"Lela," Jaroslav had squealed, covering his eyes. "You're going to make such a mess."

I had, indeed, made a mess, some of the pee landing on my skirt, but it was well worth it. I was ecstatic when the priest finally took the chalice and brought it to his lips. He must've been pretty parched from all that yapping, since he, much to my amusement, took a long, big gulp. A second or two later, the wine ended up splattered all over the altar, dripping from his chin, staining his white alb crimson.

After a few gags, his disbelief quickly turned into fury: he inspected the confused congregation with raging eyes, hands clutching the altar. I must've not contained my smug grin very well, as his eyes met mine a second too long, and at that moment I just knew that he *knew*, but in all of my victorious smugness, I didn't think much of it. After all, how would he prove it's mine, indeed?

Years later, as my lungs were filled with icy water, my mind wandered to this exact moment, wondering if my brazen attitude was a mistake. But I guessed that there was no use crying over spilled milk—or in this case—a bit of piss.

***

A year or so after the incident with the pissed sacramental wine, it was the middle of August.

White mist gathered around the field as the cold from the hills started creeping in. The bonfire rose high, burning into the night, casting a reddish hue on the damp grass. The celebration was in full swing when I finally arrived. I could hear it all the way from the village: the bawdy songs, the laughter.

I didn't really care much for the virgin Mary—she was alright, I guess, and painted very pretty on the walls of our church—but loved the theatrics of the festivity. The fire, the games, the music. The rare abundance and overindulgence in food and drink, the villagers gathered around, laughing in joy. With my stomach growling from a busy day spent at the loom, I heartily chewed on a piece of roasted pork and watched the men play tug of war, their wives cheering them on.

Once my belly was comfortably full, I slipped into the crowd of people, searching for Jaroslav and Agata. A light breeze ruffled the loose strands that fell out of my braid, tickling my face.

I eventually found Agata sitting on a ball of hay nearby, nibbling on a piece of roasted corn.

"Jaroslav left me again," she said sullenly instead of a greeting. "He took off somewhere with Petar." She spat out a charred grain of corn on the ground. The scowl on her face got deeper.

I sighed. That wasn't an uncommon occurrence. Ever since we celebrated our thirteenth birthday, our usually inseparable trio slowly drifted apart: Jaroslav started spending more time in the fields, working shoulder to shoulder with the men, as boys his age did. In the evenings they would all come back to the village, sweaty and covered in dirt, and drink while sharing stories and dirty jokes. We tried to join him, once, but he'd quickly ushered us away.

"You know that this is for men only," he'd whispered, scowling at my attempt to snatch a piece of cheese from the table.

Agata and I also had duties we needed to fulfill—she stayed at home, tending to the animals and helping her mother around the house, while I sat at the loom most days.

Sometimes, I tried to sneak to the fields and visit Jaroslav, but my mother caught me every time, already expecting my antics.

"It's not proper," mother said with a sense of finality. "You're not children anymore."

A shiver ran through Agata's hunched body. She threw the munched-on corn stalk into the grass and brought her hands around her shoulders. Her eyes were glistening in the dark, illuminated by the red licks of the bonfire.

I hated seeing her morose like that—she had the most beautiful, crooked smile, and I much preferred it to the glare she bore.

"We can have fun without them," I declared, pulling her to her feet. "Let's dance."

It took a while to warm her up to the idea. We swayed together to the rhythm of the music, the strums of the tamburica moving our limbs. My braids swung between us, long and untamed. Our arms intertwined as we spun in circles, again and again. I felt strong and invincible, my heart pounding wildly against my chest, fast and free as a sparrow on a spring's morn. Agata's silky, fair hair flew all around me, her usual coy demeanor gone—in the dark of the night, her smile was blazing and untamed, and I remember thinking, *there she is.*

After a while, we ended up in the grass, dazed and lightheaded, trying to catch a breath as laughter bubbled out of our strained lungs. The giddiness only fueled my mischief, and I found myself pulling Agata to her feet yet again.

"Come with me," I whispered into her ear. She just nodded, still woozy from our dance. She was so trusting toward me at the time, never questioning my decisions. I led her to the table and swiped a waterskin of wine, tucking it safe underneath my apron.

"Girl, put that back!" someone shouted, but I only grabbed Agata's hand and started running, sprinting across the field, stumbling into the nearby grove, finally stopping as we reached the stream. We sat by the water, catching our breath. The calm gurgle of the stream mixed with our labored breaths. We could still hear the sound of the celebration coming from the field, the music and the shouting. I took a swig of wine and passed it to Agata.

She looked a bit dubious, but still took a sip. "Will we get in trouble?" she asked, coughing into her elbow.

"What, are you scared?"

"You know my parents are strict," Agata rasped, now staring into the gurgling stream, absently fidgeting with the waterskin.

"Don't worry, I'll charm my way out of it," I assured her. She only nodded again, without any questions. How gullible we both were. "Are you still cold?" I asked, but Agata shook her head.

"No," she replied, "thank you." She took another gulp of alcohol and coughed. Her fingers skimmed the length of my braids, all the way from the roots of my hair to the small of my back. I felt my ears burn.

Her voice was soft as she spoke, lips illuminated by the pale of the moonlight. "I wish I could braid like that."

"My grandfather taught me how to do it," I replied fondly, remembering his skillful fingers and encouraging words.

"Would you braid my hair?" whispered Agata.

Of course I did. The braid, however, didn't end up perfect. My fingers, usually fearless and nimble, ran nervously through Agata's hair, fumbling at the soft strands of silk. We were so young back then, our cheeks flushed and hands hesitant.

Since that night, I've had plenty of chances to calm my fingers, and eventually, her braids came out looking smooth and beautiful and utterly perfect—gentle and shiny like the first light of dawn, or strong and resilient, like waterfalls of molten gold, weaved with all the love and affection that secretly pulsed in our chests.

***

A few years later, I was heading down the dusty path down to the stream. It was hot and humid, summer still lingering in the air, and although the moon hung high in the sky, beads of sweat were pooling at my neck. I skipped along the shadowy fields of maize, bathed dark blue in the moonlight.

It was Saturday, my favorite day. We always met on Saturdays, in those days.

However, once I arrived, a much shorter mop of blond hair waited for me. Jaroslav sat by the water, throwing pebbles into the churring flow.

It still baffled me, how fast we grew up. From a lanky and insecure boy, Jaroslav turned into a man, with shoulders broad and strong, his frame hardened by the years of labor in the fields, though his timid nature stayed.

He must've recognized the sound of my steps.

"Agata sent me to tell you that she won't be coming," he said with his back still turned. "She has to help mother with some chores." His tone was odd and distant, but I didn't read too much into it. I saw him reach for a bottle of rakija next to him, and thought, *how rude.*

"Aren't you going to share?"

I plopped down beside him, ready to snatch the bottle from his hands, but froze midway. If misery had a scent, it would be the smell of alcohol and sweat that clung onto him. His cheeks, stained with tears, were raw and red, and the pout he was sporting would have looked comical, if his eyes hadn't been so utterly anguished and pained. An owl hooted in the distance, making his hunched, shriveled form a bit ominous.

"Jaroslav," I said, and to my horror and surprise, a loud whimper came out of him. He slumped toward me and I opened my arms, cradling him like a newborn babe. It's funny that we'd both later consider this to be one of our happiest memories.

After a while, his breathing evened out. He pushed himself up and took a swig of rakija before passing it over.

"Petar is getting married," he said eventually, grabbing a few pebbles and throwing them into the stream. It seemed he avoided my eyes at all cost. "I'm also going to be expected to marry soon."

That didn't come across as surprising to me. This was just how things were around here—be born, grow up, work, marry, pop out some (preferably many, preferably male) children, and then eventually die (preferably peacefully, preferably not too soon). Many of our peers were already married, and had a couple of screaming children attached at their hips at all times.

"And so you'll marry," I replied. "What of it?"

Jaroslav let out a frustrated sigh. I was yet to experience heartbreak, so I didn't know how to recognize it at the time.

"You don't understand," he said, "I don't want to marry."

"Well, I'm not particularly keen on it myself," I confessed, and I really wasn't. I'd play the role of a crazy spinster marvelously well.

"Petar doesn't even like that girl," he murmured, not paying me much attention. Tears were pooling in his eyes again. The way he sulked, one might mistake him for a little boy instead of an almost seventeen-year-old man.

"Well, marriage doesn't have to be a union of love.

Most of them aren't," I reasoned.

He shook his head dismissively. I heard his teeth grit. The moonlight softened his wide chin, sharp cheekbones—he really did look like a boy, scared and petulant. "You don't understand," he pushed out.

"Well then, tell me and I'll understand."

"You couldn't possibly," he countered.

"Even though I'm your bestest friend in the world?"

He hesitated for a second, and I leaned in, taking his hand.

After a few moments, I felt his pungent, rakija-smelling breath on my face as he whispered in my ear.

Much to his chagrin, I busted out laughing. I never saw him that scared, not until that day in the attic years later. For a second, I thought he'd actually keel over, so I took him by the shoulders and whispered into his ear in return.

Quid pro quo. It was only fair, after all.

Jaroslav looked at me, a silly, flabbergasted expression on his face. It's unfortunate that those photography devices were not invented yet, because I would have framed it and kept it as a memory of that night.

"I'll marry you, if you want," I said, gently squeezing our clasped hands.

That owl hooted again, but now it sounded comical more than foreboding.

"I don't have a ring," is all that Jaroslav dumbly said.

"Well, you better get me one—" I shrugged "—if you want to make me your chaste and blushing bride."

He snorted. Some of the color started creeping back to his face. "You're neither chaste nor blushing, Lela," he said fondly.

"Well, of course I'm not," I agreed, "but don't let the others know that."

We walked back to the village, shoulder to shoulder, in amicable silence. The stars shone in the night sky above us, brighter than they ever had, at least to our eyes.

That night, we were both lifted of a heavy burden, and unbeknownst to us, gained a new one instead.

***

Our wedding was a joyous occasion. Mostly, we both couldn't wait to move into our own little house, and have all the privacy that we wished for.

"I didn't think I'd see the day," my mother told me as she rummaged through the house, looking for her old wedding dress. Jaroslav's parents were less excited at the prospect of welcoming a known rascal into their family, but were relieved that Jaroslav ultimately didn't resist the idea of marriage so strongly.

Agata only smiled. "Gross," was all she said, and that was all the blessing we needed.

Even to this day, I think fondly of it, even after everything that happened. I never regretted our marriage: to me, it was a testament of our defiance, a sign of our brazen search for happiness despite our circumstances.

Of course, we got married by that moronic priest. I could feel his scowl as we said our vows, crow's feet clawing at his eyes. It didn't spoil my mood, as I later found him at the celebration and shoved a glass of wine toward him.

"You should taste the wine," I told him, raising my own. "It's really good."

His silent fury exhilarated me. If looks could kill, by then I would have certainly been dead, but I couldn't care less, though, at the time.

I drained the glass with gusto. A drop of red slid from my mouth and down my neck, before finally seeping into the white of my dress.

***

Not long after, Agata got married.

A few days before the wedding, we were sitting in my workshop, as we often were. Warm rays of sunshine peeked through the pulled-up curtains. It was a nice, warm autumn afternoon, the scent of summer still lingering in the air.

Agata was leaning against the loom, watching me work on her wedding present. It was a colorful duvet, full of vertical patterns, with intricate details making out floral shapes. In the center of it was a small heart, hidden between a row of delicate daisies. The duvet was supposed to be a surprise, but we never could keep secrets from each other for long.

"This won't change a thing," Agata said to me that day. When her hand came to rest on my shoulder, I reveled in the warmth it left on my skin.

We had many conversations about her upcoming marriage—before, and then after the wedding—but the conclusion was always the same: there was nothing to be done. It was the way it needed to be, and Tomislav, her husband-to-be, seemed like a nice enough man, at least at that time.

I stopped weaving and took Agata's hand.

"I know that, dear heart," I told her, pressing a kiss into the gentle skin of her palm. It's still nice, sometimes, to remember just how in love I was. My heart pounded strong and unapologetic back then, and loved just as much.

That's why I pulled Agata's hand to my chest, to show her what lay inside.

"How would it?" I asked her, feeling her clever fingers undo the buttons of my shirt.

After a while, I went back to weaving, and Agata took her place by the window.

Even though I can't feel it now, it's still nice to remember, sometimes, what lovesick fools we were.

***

Sometime later, it was early spring.

We were sitting by the stream, leaning against each other. Spring was my favorite time of year, but today, even the prettiest flower that popped out of the dewey grass annoyed me. I tried to savor this moment we had together, as they'd gotten sparser, but I just couldn't.

"This still won't change a thing," Agata assured me, idly stroking my hair. I buried my face in her neck, unable to meet her eyes; I hated being scared, being a coward. I didn't want her to see the tears that threatened to spill down my cheeks, or the sorry wobble of my lips, because I knew it was silly of me, of course. That's how things were, back then—there was nothing to be done. I knew this was bound to happen, but still, it felt like the worst kind of betrayal.

I looked down at her belly. She was going to start showing, soon.

"You'll make a wonderful mother," I said to her, ignoring the pang in my chest.

I haven't braided her hair in quite some time.

***

"Auntie Lela, mother sent me to pick up the eggs for the cake!" I heard Antun shout. A moment later, he barged into my workshop and pushed a basket into my arms.

I smiled at Agata's son, at his ruddy cheeks and soft, ruffled hair. He had his mother's blue eyes and, unfortunately, his father's loud and demanding demeanor, but I loved him nonetheless, like all of Agata's children. Of course I did. There were four of them, now, two boys and two girls, and one more on the way.

Together, we headed to the chicken coop. I let Antun pick out the biggest, shiniest eggs, and then threw in some fresh zlevka that Jaroslav had baked that morning. That was what my love was reduced to at the time: veiled acts of service such as a dozen eggs, a few slices of sweet bread, and a stolen moment in my workshop, if we were lucky.

Antun thanked me before running off back home. It was his birthday, and a big celebration was in the works. He was the eldest son, after all. I wasn't particularly keen on going, as these celebrations were starting to get tiring, but I knew it meant a great deal to Agata, and she did mean a great deal to me.

More and more unwarranted questions had started coming my way—about my marriage, about the children I had yet to birth. People loved to gossip, and the state of my womb was a hot topic. Jaroslav would stifle a laugh every time he overheard some of his noisy relatives try to elicit some intriguing detail about our intimate life from me, but lately, even his shoulders had started to tense at the subject.

That day was no exception. A swarm of overzealous aunties surrounded me like a pack of wolves. I was alone and defenseless against their probing, as Jaroslav had disappeared somewhere with his new best friend, Matej, and I barely got a glimpse of Agata, who was busy playing a happy wife and tending to her needy children.

Which was alright, of course it was.

I drank a few shots of rakija, and then some more. Eventually, the curious horde moved on to another unlucky individual, discouraged by my uninformative, derisive answers, and soon, a girl sat next to me, sighing wistfully into her wine, complaining how unhappy she was with her life in the village.

I wasn't even aware at the time whom I was talking to. Admittedly, I was really drunk, and the girl, well, she was drunk as a skunk too.

"You should try to leave, then," I told her, sincere and passionate in my drunken state. Around us, men chortled and women huffed and puffed and children screamed, but as I caught Agata's eyes for a moment in the screaming mass, all of the noise went away.

The things we do for love. I turned to the girl and clinked our glasses together. Drink made me real sappy, sometimes. "Do what makes you happy," I said to her, overcome with emotion.

She nodded enthusiastically and tipped our glasses before she spoke again. "Did you ever thought about leaving this place?"

"No," I answered truthfully.

"Why?"

"I fell in love here," I replied simply. It's hard to believe how naive I was at the time, but I never knew any other way to be, not until I was born again.

A few days later, the girl, who happened to be Agata's sister-in-law, took my advice and left the village, sneaking out in the dead of night. She didn't get very far, though, as her father tracked her down quickly and dragged her back home. Her family was furious. Tomislav was fuming, Agata told me later.

I don't think she told anyone about our conversation, but she might as well, since, from that day on, the villagers started looking at me with suspicion. The village was scandalized, much like the priest had been when I pissed in his wine. I'd already cultivated a reputation as an unusual woman—childless, often stealing my husband's clothes, regularly skipping Sunday Mass.

"Did you really tell her to do that?" Agata asked me the next time we were alone. I rarely got to see her this unguarded toward me anymore, without her husband's hand at the small of her back, or a bunch of children tugging at her apron. At the time, I was foolish enough to think of it as jealousy.

She was starting to get nervous, and I was starting to get resentful, but it never crossed my mind, not for a moment, that things might escalate the way they did.

***

Jaroslav was starting to get antsy, too.

"You should bear my child soon," he said to me one day as we sat in the garden, drinking tea and watching the sun rise.

I huffed, annoyed. I loved the mornings we spent together in companionable silence, watching the hills slowly light up with the first light of dawn.

"That's awfully threatening," I joked and hoped we would leave it at that, but Jaroslav turned to me, brow furrowed and pleading. I almost laughed at how expectant he looked.

"It's just that my family is starting to have questions," he whispered like it was a secret, like I would gasp in shock, or the chickens would scurry around in their coop at his admission.

I knew that, of course. After all, we were approaching the tenth year of our marriage with no children to show, and what an abnormality that was, at that time. Hushed whispers would follow us as we strolled through the village—the two of us, without a child plastered to my hip or mounted atop his shoulders. What an odd sight that was.

In the beginning, the fuss amused me more than it irked me. By that point I'd already been lying to various midwives for years: their advice went disobeyed and their herbs burned in the fireplace. *Yes, yes, thank you*, I blabbed and later snickered, once out of their earshot, sure that the topic would die out eventually, but it never did—not even the bloody rags we tried to pass off as miscarriages were enough to stop people from prattling about the sorry state of my poor womb.

"Why do they assume that I'm the problem?" I often grumbled to an amused Jaroslav as yet another one of his aunts backed me into a corner and bestowed me with yet another piece of unsolicited advice on how to keep the husband happy and satisfied.

To others, I appeared old and fruitless. A bit frigid, maybe, which made Agata and I laugh in private. I received countless pitiful glances thrown my way, at my flat belly and dry bosom. But ironically, I was full of life and joy.

For someone to assume my body was desolate and barren was an insult. Did I really need to push out a child to appear whole?

"Please," Jaroslav said that day. "Just think about it."

To be honest, I wasn't even that opposed to a child. I just detested being told what to do—by my pushy in-laws, the presumptuous villagers, that stupid priest, and, admittedly, even Jaroslav and Agata.

We both went back to our cups in silence. A wind started to blow, timid at first, then forceful and cold. It grazed my bare arms and a violent shiver that ran through me caught me by surprise. Soon, the first light of dawn was extinguished by the glum, heavy clouds. The air smelled of the upcoming rain, and something else I couldn't recognize. It made me oddly unsettled, looking at the hills that stretched before us, now dark and dismal. Where did the golden treetops go, all of a sudden?

"I think it'll rain soon," was all I said, and Jaroslav hummed, or maybe it was the wind whispering instead.

Something sour slithered its way between us, and for the first time since we stepped into the church and said our vows, something unpleasant coiled in my stomach. Suddenly, our house felt as if made of glass, and the village too small and too suffocating, its familiar paths leading into a never-ending circle.

***

It was a rough year. Spring was wet and rainy, and the summer, as if out of sheer spite, was dry and fruitless and miserable. The crops failed, the earth dry and barren.

The winter that came after was harsh and unforgiving, the coldest one in years. A fever ran through the village in waves, flourishing among the weakened and malnourished bodies, brutal and deadly, leaving many frozen graves in its wake. In desperation, people prayed and prayed, but nothing came of it—their stomachs remained empty and their loved ones buried under icy soil.

"Have faith," the priest preached every Sunday, but the words had to have rung untrue even to his arrogant ears. Misery made the villagers untrusting and waspish toward him. People needed something—or someone—to blame, to rage at, to point their fingers and scream: *Here's the culprit!*

"Have faith," the priest swore—but his promise of a better future seemed hollow and meaningless as a dried-up well.

Piety was running low without anything tangible, anything corporal, and in hindsight, the priest must have known that.

My loom was consequently the busiest it had ever been, providing thick blankets and warm capes for the wintry cold. With stiff fingers I mended holes and seams, worked by the fire until the dead of night, when the only sound was the snow falling softly onto the cold ground.

Even to me, ever the optimist, joy was hard to find during those months. Just like the rest of the village, I too, was agitated: going to bed with nothing but the cold pinching at my skin, a growling stomach, and the scent of misery hanging in the air, sharp and sour.

So I sat by the loom, having nothing else to do. I weaved, and then weaved more, the days blending into a continuous hank of thread and yarn.

That's why I'd forgotten what day it was that particular day, until I heard a familiar rap of knocks against the door. I was by them in an instant, as if pulled by an invisible rope.

It was Saturday, my favorite day.

"It's been so long," I said, yanking Agata inside.

"I know, I know," she replied, frozen lips tickling my neck.

Back then, even in the bleakest moments, there was still a beacon of light, here or there.

Later, as we lay embraced on our makeshift bed by the loom, Agata shook her head.

"I forgot to bring the bread," she sighed. Every time we met like this, it was under the guise of a cordial family visit, bringing over some treats she liked to bake.

"No worries," I reassured her, "I suppose it's too moldy and hard to even bite." The joke fell flat, because that was, in fact, the truth.

Agata's stare was vacant, so I pulled her closer.

"I don't know where my head is, these days," she mumbled, buried in the crook of my neck.

My palm came around her blushing cheek. "It's right here, dear heart," I whispered, although deep down, I knew she was right. It had been like this for quite some time now, and I didn't want to admit back then, but her withdrawal had started long before that impending moment in that wretched attic.

The gentle words I whispered into the shell of her ear didn't seem to comfort her.

"Our parents are starting to itch for Jaroslav's grandchildren," she said instead, rolling to the other side of the covers. The cold seeped in immediately, shaking me to my bones.

"They have plenty already," I bit back by reflex, not proud of the venom that slipped through my voice. As I've said, the cold and the hunger had made me irritable, and if I knew that this would be the last time we spoke, I would've chosen to instead embrace Agata once again as tightly as I could.

Agata shook her head, as if scolding me. I hated when she did that, like I was one of her snotty children. "You already have a reputation. People talk."

"I thought you loved that about me," I teased, or pleaded even, trying to lighten the mood, but Agata didn't bite.

"We're not children anymore," was all she told me, fumbling with a loose thread sticking out of the cover, and ripped the seam.

We bickered like that for some time back and forth, the cold and hunger momentarily forgotten. We were so consumed by our grievances, the grudges that we swore we didn't hold against each other, that we didn't notice that our usual one-hour time slot was long over, or, more importantly, Agata's husband staring at us from the small, fogged window, the forgotten bread squished in his hands.

***

Jaroslav walked in front of me, furiously pacing down the path.

"Jaroslav," I called out. It was hard to keep up in the snowstorm. We passed the town square, empty and desolate. It was far too cold to be outside, but we'd been called to visit Jaroslav's parents, without the option to decline. Antun came by earlier that morning to tell us we were expected. We barely recognized him, with how the scowl twisted his young face.

He spat on our doorstep before disappearing into the blizzard.

The snow squeaked beneath our boots, nearly knee high. I almost slipped. The wet cloth of my dress clung uncomfortably to my long undergarments. Frustration shook my insides.

"Jaroslav!" I shouted, agitated. "Would you please slow down for a moment?"

He turned around, eyes wide and furious. Some lone villagers passed us by, sending curious glances our way, intrigued by our unusual public marital dispute—after all, our marriage was seemingly among the harmonious ones in the village.

His childish behavior annoyed me. I didn't like how he concealed his fear with fury. *Toughen up*, I wanted to say, but I knew it wouldn't be fair. *We'd made it so far*, I thought, as the cold winds whipped our faces, but Jaroslav only glowered and huffed and sniveled, much like he did that night by the river, almost a decade ago.

"You've put us all at risk," he'd said last night while pulling the covers over us, and then turned his back to me. Only a few feet had been between us, but it might've as well been an ocean. By then, I knew how to read every frown of his brow, every tense muscle in his shoulders, every silence he was unwilling to break, and this one meant: *I'm scared, and you're to blame.*

I was not blind to the consequences we were to face. I knew he was worried about what his parents would think, what they would say, how they would look at us; he was worried about Tomislav's bad temper and clenched fists; he was worried about what the other villagers might say about me, and how it would reflect upon him; and in the end, he was worried about the future of his relationship with Matej, his beloved.

Ever since I'd confessed to him what happened the day before, how Tomislav furiously pounded down the workshop door and silently waited for Agata to finish dressing, that was what's been going through Jaroslav's head.

"It's going to be alright," I told him there, in the heart of a snowstorm, and meant it. I had no idea what was waiting for us at his parents' house, but I was too untroubled and reckless to imagine the worst. Without a doubt, a scolding was ahead. Yelling, screaming, crying. Appalled glares and mouths wrinkled in distaste. Maybe, if someone felt frisky, some holy water would end up being splashed on my face. I could take that. It'll blow over in a few days, anyway, I remember reasoning with myself.

Jaroslav didn't seem convinced, nor consoled by my words. After a few moments, though, his hand found mine in the cold.

I placed a frozen kiss on his prickly cheek. "In good times and in bad, right?"

We continued our way against the icy winds.

***

The house was silent upon our arrival. We found Jaroslav's grandmother alone at the common room table. A pile of meat lay in front of her, fresh and bloody. The whole room reeked of copper. She put the knife down and wiped her hands against the red-stained apron around her waist. The wind still howled outside.

"You stupid children," she whispered, rubbing hands against her temples. She fished out a rosary from her apron, wrapped it around her bony wrist and began slicing the meat before speaking again. "They are in the attic," she told us gravely and started muttering prayers under her breath.

I suppressed a laugh at her dramatic display and Jaroslav elbowed me in the ribs. We would've thought it strange, that they'd slaughtered one of their last animals before we came, but we were preoccupied with other things. It was hard to connect the dots, back then.

Jaroslav took my hand and led us to the attic. Once we climbed up, though, some of my merry-go-lucky attitude wavered.

The attic was dim and dusty, illuminated by a few candles placed on the wooden floor. It was a small room, and it stank of iron and incense. The smell made me nervous. Something sinister lingered in the air, contained in the walls of the room.

Once my eyes adjusted to the darkness, I saw the priest's face glowering in the shadows. *Great.* There would be holy-water splashing after all. Jaroslav's parents and Agata and Tomislav were there too, paired at the priest's sides. I searched Agata's face, but her eyes were glued to the floor. I still felt assured, the lovesick fool that I was.

I sighed, feeling Jaroslav squirm beside me. Nobody moved, nobody talked. The silence was oppressing, and back then, I was never good at keeping quiet. All this dramatic fanfare, just because two people dared to love each other.

So I spoke. In my impatience, I didn't even notice the wooden bucket that was placed right in front of us.

"Hello," I said, flashing my best innocent smile. I should've just run until my legs gave out instead. It would have saved me a lot of grief. And yet I remained right there, in that putrid attic, ready to look them in the eyes.

It all happened so fast, after that.

In the blink of an eye, Tomislav rushed toward us and tackled Jaroslav to the ground, the reassuring warmth of his hand in mine gone. Somebody screamed; I can't recall if it was myself, or maybe Agata, but whoever did, it was a primal, guttural scream, a scream of foreshadowing.

Adrenaline rushed through me and I was ready to throw myself on the floor as well; I was looking for a valid excuse to smack Agata's husband anyway. But before I could claw at Tomislav's back, callous hands gripped me by the neck, pulling me toward the center of the room.

Jaroslav's father breathed at my neck like a bull. My knees buckled, and they hit the wooden floor with a dull thud. For a second my vision went white, but soon the face of the priest appeared in front of me. His eyes shone with wicked anticipation.

What a beast he was.

"In the Name of the Father, and of the Son, and of the Holy Ghost," he trembled as he spoke. "Amen."

His words echoed around the attic. A storm raged inside me, much like the blizzard we'd stumbled through to get here, wild and ravenous, and I knew I couldn't do much to contain it. I always hated how high and mighty the priest sounded, and then, as I kneeled before him, the harsh, ragged wood scraping the skin from my knees like the corn did all those years ago, fury clouded my head. I knew this wasn't good, wasn't good at all, but I just couldn't help myself.

The bucket stood before me, filled with water. I laughed.

"Are you about to wash my feet?" I asked, savoring every word like it was the most delicious meal I could think of. "If so, I must warn you—they're real dirty.

Might take you a while to get it all."

Seconds later, my head was pushed into the bucket. Cold water flooded my nostrils, splashed my neck. A violent shiver seized my body as I trashed against the iron grip around my head.

Air had never felt so good, once I was pulled back from the water. My lungs heaved, and my nails were torn and bloodied from all the scraping.

"Repent for your sins," I heard the priest say somewhere above me. A crucifix was shoved into my face. I did the only thing that I could think of. I spat on it.

"Fuck you," I added, for good measure.

It went on like that for a while. Words left my frenzied mouth every time they could: *you won't get away with this, I'll strangle you with your stupid rosary, I'm glad I pissed in your wine*. In my rage, I could've gone like this for hours more.

Though my ears rang and buzzed and shrilled, I could hear Jaroslav and Tomislav still wrestling in the back, and my mother-in-law muttering prayers under her breath, but through all the noise and grunts and clamor, it was Agata's silence I heard the loudest.

"It's no use," the priest said after a while. For a moment, it appeared his efforts were finally over, but his tone was more smug than defeated. He turned to Jaroslav's mother and silently jerked his head. She scurried downstairs without hesitation.

I wonder how much any of them knew.

A small flame of hope ignited in me as I saw Agata grab something long, a hoe or a rake. *C'mon*, I urged her silently, *please*. She still didn't look at me, but I would forgive her, of course I would, when she swung and smashed the priest's head into a bloody pulp.

Blunt fingers squeezed my neck. My vision blurred

until all I could see was the priest's victorious face. It finally dawned on me, at that point, what I was: the perfect scapegoat to his cause, his dying influence, his need for fearmongering—lo and behold, the devil that's walking among us, wicked and nasty and foul. I will seduce their daughters, trick their sons, deprive them of their grandchildren. I'll suck out all the life from their soil, and nothing will be left, except a land barren and desolate.

Anguish choked me. A strange chant was beginning to be sung—it was different from those recited among the halls of the church, and I knew that was for a reason. I pleaded silently to Agata, pleaded for her to have the courage that I desperately hoped she had inside of her.

My head hit the water again. This time, it lasted longer. The whispers were right all those years ago, after all. A man of God, a man of the Devil—what difference did it make, in the end? I didn't know where he'd learned the words that he chanted, or who they belonged to, but that didn't matter, as they were spoken by a weak and vengeful man, a man with vain pride and no morals.

Stupid, stupid priest, I sniveled into the bucket.

The attic ladder squeaked. Once my head was free again, I found Agata gone, the tool she'd been gripping lying on the floor.

Her mother passed the priest something hard and long, wrapped in a crimson-stained cloth. The sour, rusty stench of iron assaulted my nostrils again, stronger than before. My limbs sagged from exhaustion, and my head felt so heavy I thought I'd snap my neck if the harsh hands pulling at my hair disappeared.

Later, I tormented myself. Why didn't I fight harder? I searched for a different answer every time as I wandered the foggy hills, but the conclusion was always the same:

it was hard to fight for something that wouldn't fight back for you.

The flame snuffed out, and I finally learned what heartbreak felt like.

Foul, foul, foul, it rang against my ears, against the walls of the attic. The floor underneath me trembled, the water boiled, the wind outside wailed. *Foul*, it rang everywhere.

That was my last thought, as a searing pain burst in my head, and everything went to black.

***

I was woken up to rough hands under my armpits, which hoisted me upright.

My legs trembled underneath me. I wasn't sure where I was, at first, or what happened. My lungs strained with every breath I took—it felt like being burned inside, and my head didn't feel any better. It pulsed, throbbed, banged in the same meter as the heartbeat in my throat: loud and forceful, disorienting and nauseating. Something dripped down my forehead and into my eyes. I saw nothing but red.

"Stop it," I wheezed to the harsh hands which now clutched my sides, but they only pushed harder.

Slowly, the town square came into focus. The blizzard had finally calmed down and the villagers stood around, bewildered. Every now and then, a lone snowflake would land on my cheek, swirling from the gray sky.

For a few moments, there was nothing in the air except the ugly sounds of my ragged breath, until a scream came behind me. The grip around my ribs tightened, and a yelp came and died in my throat.

"Behold the devil that has walked among us," the priest roared, "that has cursed our land!"

His words rang against my ears. I was sure I'd go deaf. *Shut up, stupid priest*, I thought, but of course he didn't. Men like him never did.

"She'll eat our children, defile our women!" he continued, and pushed me forward. This time, I landed on the ground again, limbs sliding against the ice. My head was awfully heavy and my ears buzzed like crazy.

Still, I heard the gasps, heard the whispers. The horror, the fear, the hunger, and at last—the blame. They feasted on it, enjoyed it, letting it nourish their starved bodies and entranced minds. Sunday Mass looked a bit different that day.

"Devil woman," the villagers screamed, "harlot!"

"Witch!"

"Godless wench!"

In a different context, those names would make me laugh, but now they stung like a stake through the heart—I hated not having the last word, and by then, it didn't matter what I said either way.

"Babaroga!" someone shouted, coining the name that would cling to me for centuries, and remind me of the harsh hands on the back of my head, the searing burn in my lungs, and all the things I'd lost in that stinking attic.

I barely saw the villagers as I stumbled past them. Their faces were grotesque and blurry, and I tried not to look at them, distantly aware of the few missing this spectacle. My mother might have been there, pale and rigid amongst the crowd, but she also might have not.

"All the hard labor, and this is what I get?" I thought I'd heard her say, but I also might had not. My head was a swirl of pain and confusion, and it was hard to think of anything other than that splitting headache.

Rotten fruit hit my face, splattered against my body.

"Idiots," I muttered, "keep the little food you have," but I might've only thought it.

Hands, big and small ones, pushed me along the path, lifting me up when I slipped or fell—I had no other choice than to keep walking ahead, wobbling beside the gray, barren fields, until I was out of the village.

It was apparent to me that there was no going backward. With a heavy head, and an even heavier heart, I walked until my legs finally gave out.

***

I was lying next to the stream when I came to. A wave of queasiness hit me, and I coughed up some saliva. It tasted of iron. My head still throbbed with pain, pulsing in my brow, and I knew I couldn't stall anymore.

It took a massive effort to lift my hand and slide my fingers over the hard, bony mass. It was bumpy and sharp, and I stopped before my torn nails could catch on its ridges.

The pile of fresh meat, the pointed, red-stained cloth her mother-in-law had obediently handed over to the priest, the sinister chants—it all spun in my head. My chest started to heave. I didn't even try to stop the next bout of nausea.

I'm not sure how long I lay there in the snow, surrounded by my own sick. Tears slid silently across my cheeks, each one stinging my skin in the cold. It was hard to imagine that only yesterday I wished Jaroslav a good morning, and later rushed to meet Agata at the door.

I began to realize that time wouldn't mean anything to me anymore.

Familiar footsteps squeaked against the snow. I turned my head to the side and met his eyes. For a while, we just looked at each other. He didn't come close. There was a bruise blooming on his cheek, and his left eye was purple and swollen like a plum.

He spoke first, this time. "I have to escort you to your lair," Jaroslav said, and I blinked.

Lair? I looked helplessly at him as though he'd grown a second head, and I weren't stuck with a goatlike horn plastered to the front of mine. I tried to frown, but it hurt too much. What about our warm little house, our chicken coop, my workshop? But my throat was like a dried-up well, and the questions never reached the surface. I staggered to my feet, doing my best to stifle the yelps of pain—I was desperate for the comforting warmth of his palm against mine.

"I can't come with you," Jaroslav continued, and pointed to the hills with a shaky hand. "He said you'll recognize it once you see it." It was then that his voice broke, and he turned his head to the side, away from me and my nasty, stupid horn.

I was about to reach out, but finally realized there was a reason we stood apart, and that it wasn't me who was keeping it so.

"I'm sorry," he whispered. "This was not what I wanted."

I blinked again. *Oh, cry me a river,* I wanted to snap back, but a strangled sob came out instead.

I wanted to scream at Jaroslav, at his stupid, God-fearing parents. I wanted to run back to the village and stab that fucking priest through the chest and show him what a devil really looks like. I wanted to scream at the naive villagers and pelt them with rotten vegetables like they had me. Anger was like a restless beast hidden inside my chest, clawing its way out, until I remembered the sound of Agata's steps rushing down the ladder, and suddenly, all the searing, unbearable fury disappeared.

Shame crept on me. My mother was right—I only brought trouble, and I didn't even manage to fulfill my grandfather's dying wishes. My arms were dangling limply at my sides, red-stained and stiff. I took a glance at the fields of white, at the village that spread behind them. What was it that I'd said to Tomislav's sister? *I fell in love here*, I'd told her, the gullible, lovesick woman that I was. Bitterness took over, souring my breath. It burned my tongue, slithered its way down my throat and enveloped my lungs, until it finally reached my heart.

Without any parting words, I turned around and walked. The hills rose in front of me, white and solid, and Jaroslav was right. Somehow, I knew exactly where to go.

If my memory isn't mistaken, I think I heard Jaroslav call out my name, but maybe it was just wishful thinking. Whatever the case may be, I didn't turn back.

It was hard to walk—the horn kept throwing me off balance, and I stumbled many times on my journey until I was accustomed to the incongruous mass weighing me down. The cape I wore was wet and dirty, dragging heavy against the frozen ground. The forest slowly turned darker, and I welcomed the gloom. Fog gathered around the edges, swallowing the trees, and soon I was walking through a gray haze, murky and somber as my mind was.

My breath became shorter with each step I took. I panted and wheezed like a wild animal. When I thought my body couldn't take any more, I stuck my hand in the nearest bush and rummaged through it until I found a firm branch, and I continued to hobble my way up.

Finally, my feet led me to a small meadow, which backed against the bottom of a hill. It was white and cold and frozen, and I knew that I was at the right place. A lonesome foyer to my new home. There was a faint light at the far end of it, a small crack in the stone, narrow and almost invisible, and I crossed the foggy field toward the slit of muted, orange haze.

Once in the cave, I stuck my frozen hands out to the fire that burned inside it. I was barely able to feel a lick of warmth before it snuffed out. So I lay there in the darkness, listening to the sound of the water dripping against the stones, until the beat of my heart ceased.

There on the damp ground I was born again, as the horned creature named Babaroga.

***

I rarely ventured outside the cave. I didn't have the need to eat or drink, piss or shit. Most days were spent lying in the dark, and staring at the rugged, stone ceiling. I only ever left my cave in the dead of night. Cloaked in my worn mantle, I would roam the forest silently and aimlessly for hours, for days, for months. If I'd still been mortal, there would have been no skin or muscle left in the soles of my feet, only bone as white as the moon that shone above me.

I was always careful to come back before dawn. Sunshine irritated me immensely.

"Stupid, stupid sun," I would spit at the sky, but the sun wasn't at fault for being the sun, no more than I was for becoming the creature that I became.

Sometimes, in those early years, I descended down past the maize fields. People still talked, whispered, gossiped. Another wave of sickness made its way through the village, and while it left the priest dead and frozen under a pile of cold ground, his words still echoed in the minds of the villagers. Fear of my devious nature slithered around like a poisonous snake. That was the point, after all—I only served one purpose, and apparently, I did it well with little to no effort.

If I could, if my body hadn't dried up like it had, I'd take a piss on the priest's grave. Just for good measure, of course.

I'd walk silently across the village, dust rising at my feet. I'd move like a wraith, creep across the square, lurk in the backyards, until women would shriek and men curse in fear.

"Babaroga!" they'd scream. They'd clasp their hands in prayers, wave rosaries in my direction, and the bravest ones even pelted me with rocks. Sometimes, I bared my teeth at them with a wicked grin just for fun, but my heart wasn't really in it. Mischief didn't bring me joy anymore. What good would it do, when I didn't have a heartbeat to rile up, to fill me up with that sweet rush of provocation?

Through generations, my story became adorned: my makeshift staff became a broom which I flew on, cackling and shrieking like a wild fox, and my big, voracious stomach growled for children I devoured with my ragged teeth. Later, I would spew their little skulls around the entrance of my cave, meat still clinging to my red gums.

Apparently, I became ugly too, and about half a decade older. I was hunchbacked, horrifyingly devious and crooked, with hairy moles all over my face, and a big, bumpy nose, sharp as a knife. I suppose Agata's husband started that rumor. Idiot.

I never peeked into their houses. I couldn't bear to see how Jaroslav, Agata or my mother stood—or didn't—to live without me. The urge wasn't strong anyway. I was a monster, and monsters didn't feel.

Years later, as I took one of my last walks down to the village, I stumbled upon their graves. A distant memory resurfaced in my head, about how I wished to be buried next to them when our time came. Memories long forgotten came to life, vivid in the hazy moonlight: the way that Jaroslav's laugh filled our house, or the way that Agata's head perfectly fit in the crook of my neck. My anger might've died in that cave, but apathy took its place. Even if I tried to smile, it would look like nothing but a grimace.

I didn't linger long. The sun was about set, and I still had a long way up the mountains.

***

Time went by. If asked, I couldn't tell how many years have passed since I've climbed up the hills.

The legend slowly died down, reduced only to a scary bedtime story for naughty children. People still ran in the other direction as our paths crossed, but as times changed, I'd diminished to a shadow lost between the trees, a trick of the eye. Nobody took me seriously anymore. The idiot priest would turn in his grave if he knew. All his hard work gone to waste.

Although I didn't venture into the village anymore,

I could tell, of course, that things were different—I will never forget the first time I heard the bang of a hunting rifle, or the rumble of a car. The night became richer with shining satellites and airplane tracks, and I found myself often staring at the sky, watching their glimmer in the mass of dark.

Sometimes, I lingered around the hikers, overheard their talks. There were many things I didn't understand anymore, but I caught up fairly quickly. Plastic children's toys, pills, mobile phones, nice smelling books, metal water bottles, thinly sliced, crunchy potatoes stuffed inside of a wrinkly bag—it was fascinating what people left behind. Some of it I took back to my cave. I inspected it, played with it, tried it on. I liked a certain pair of heavy, red boots, so I kept those on. They were sturdy and nice looking, and I loved to crunch twigs and dry leaves under their soles. It wasn't such a bad time to be alive, if I were really alive. Sometimes, I took a fancy glass bottle of a nice smelling liquid and sprayed it across the cave, across my neck and robe, across the pile of stuff I accumulated over the years.

When boredom got the best of me, I flipped through some newspapers and magazines, stared at the words until I learned how to make sense of them. They were soggy and moldy from the dampness of the cave, and I still didn't understand a whole lot of it, but the colorful pages were welcomed in the quiet dark around me.

I was reading through a beauty magazine when I found a text titled *10 Ways to Stop Aging*. I huffed and puffed and shook my head. I couldn't fathom it.

"Stupid people," I said and flipped the page. Aging was a privilege. I'd give anything to break this curse, to make time work for me again. A while ago, I found a thrown-out cup in the forest. *Every Day Is a Second Chance* was written on it. It was dumb, as I knew that every day certainly wasn't a new chance, but for some reason, I still took it to my cave.

Sometimes, I would stop by the stream. It didn't look much like before, now that trash cans and benches had popped up beside it, but I would sit there in the dead of the night, thinking about the dull eternity that stretched before me.

I never stayed long. The gurgle of water would start to agitate me, and I would claw the bench underneath me until I'd remember my torn nails, scraped against that bucket of water.

I scratched away like that until my mind would go blank again. There was no harm in it—what's a few scratches here and there?

I was sure nobody would notice it, anyways.

***

I was out on my nightly stroll when I saw the girl. She lay in the mud, unconscious. Blood slid down her forehead, and I stopped dead in my tracks. The sight struck me. I had no excuse to bring her back to the cave—maybe that should've been the first clue. It would have been easier to move her near a lodge or a street, and let somebody else take care of her. What was it to me, to pick her up and cradle her to my chest?

But I cleaned her face, dressed her wounds. There was no sanity as my fingers weaved a delicate braid into her damp hair. "It's alright," I told her as she trashed in her delirious state, though she predictably fled in horror once she woke up. I couldn't blame her—I was a horned monster, and she was a concussed, bleeding woman. The optics weren't great.

But then she came back. *What a strange creature*, I thought, which was rich, coming from me. She had more courage than her apprehensive demeanor led on. I could tell she was restless and scared, but there was something else there, something else hidden beneath her nervous stares and fidgety hands—a heart she had yet to discover—and I was envious. She had so much in front of her, and I had nothing else but a cave as desolate as my heart.

It was strange, the way we fell into conversation. I forgot how nice it was to talk, to hear and be heard. Maybe, if it weren't for the horn, and her conflicted nature—well. It was nice to let my mind wander for a second.

Still, I was weary. Nobody would just stumble back to my cave out of sheer politeness, so I did the only sensible thing I could think of, and sent her off to the lodge.

You've been nothing but lovely this evening, she told me before we parted. I could've sworn I felt my cheeks flush and my nonexistent breath hitch. That should've been the second clue, if I were looking for one. Ever since our paths had crossed, there was this prickly sensation underneath my skin, warm and buzzing, but it must've been a fluke, a last twitch of my dead, rotten nervous system.

Who are you? she demanded next, trembling in front of my face, so close and trusting, and I couldn't bring myself to answer her question. Who was I, indeed? Ever since she'd stumbled back to the cave, it seemed that neither of us had a clue. The dart that flew to my neck seconds later seemed to say, *a monster, that needs to be hunted*. The prick of the needle surprised me, as I hadn't felt any pain since I'd climbed up the hills. It was awfully familiar, though, when that dart struck me. I'd prefer the rotten fruit, to be honest.

As I woke up on the table in the lodge, instinct tugged at me, red-hot and ravenous, and I let myself be led with a newfound joy. I never used my horn for monstrous things, but then I thought, *here's a monster, if you so desperately wish to see one*. I didn't even question the morality of the bloodshed. Something in me knew it had been a long time coming.

Those drawings of my face were unpleasant, I'll admit, even after hearing and laughing at the false depiction of my appearance through the years. But my limbs still moved with strength I hadn't felt for centuries, and I poked and clawed and bashed with fervor. I could feel my long forgotten need for mischief stir, my buried, deep ache for revenge rise to the surface, ferocious and unforgiving.

The bloodied mischief led me back to water. Life's cruel like that. My body, so free and feral only seconds ago, froze as soon as I landed into that ridiculous bubbling tub. I could almost smell the attic again, taste the iron; my chest even heaved and choked, and I would have found that incredibly strange, if I hadn't been so struck by the long forgotten memories that gripped my limbs.

This time, though, a pair of resolute hands came to lift me up, and I coughed and heaved until my lungs ached with pain.

That would've been the third clue, if I were counting.

Watching that awful woman be drowned was really comforting. *Confront your demons*, popped up in my head. I think I read that, somewhere, in a mildewy magazine.

I pulled Kaja from the water, and when our eyes met, I knew that she'd finally found the heart she'd so badly hidden away from.

The brush of her lips felt sobering. The bright chirping of the birds around us, the gentle rustle of the treetops, the soft, salty skin of her cheek—suddenly, my senses were overwhelmed, and I felt everything, everything and so much more, felt it as clear and bright as a gurgling stream on a summer's day.

Then, another girl flew out the door, and there was screaming and crying and hugging, but surprisingly, not a lot of fear. I let them squabble and lifted a hand to my chest.

The morning wind blew, crisp and sharp. Something crinkled by my feet, amongst the leaves and blood and muck. I glanced down at the paper and smiled.

Bye-Bye, Babaroga, it read.

The thump of my heart was steady and unyielding. Life spread in front of me after hundreds of years, shining with the first lights of dawn.

Epilogue

THERE'S A REST STOP at the foot of the Kalnik mountain, with a stream hidden behind a birch forest. Every few months, a girl strolls through the trees and plops a heavy backpack on the wooden bench.

She doesn't stick around for long, just enough to jot down a message on a piece of paper and stick it in the backpack. *My salon's doing well, business is blooming, always happy to feed you. xoxo P.S. nobody still has a clue. the latest bet is a unicorn. idiots*, the most recent one read. She drives off before the night falls.

When the fog starts to gather around the stream, and the moon hangs high in the sky, a figure descends from the hills. She lets herself sit on the bench for a while before picking up the backpack with a smile hidden in the hood of her jacket. She also doesn't linger much. It's a long way back up to the top of the hills, where a cave is waiting for her.

A cave with a horn, and two brave, beating hearts.

ACKNOWLEDGMENTS

Firstly, I would like to thank you, dear reader, for picking up this book and giving it a chance. You've made my day, and I can only hope you've had a good time reading it.

Secondly, I would like to thank my editor, Vesna Kurilić, for her valuable input and ongoing support during the creation of this book—the process of writing and editing was much more seamless with her assistance and encouragement. Thank you for helping me bring Babaroga back to life.

To Antonija Mežnarić, for inspiring me to write speculative fiction and introducing me to the world of queer horror through her short story collection Mistress of Geese, and her other fantastic work. Please do check her writing if you're into queer horror inspired by Slavic folklore—it's nothing short of amazing. You can find her on IG at @antonijamezni.

A combined thank you goes to Vesna and Antonija, aka Shtriga Books: thank you for giving me the opportunity to type this project into life; this book wouldn't have been possible without you and I'm immensely grateful for your trust, as well as your friendship.

A huge thank you goes to my wonderful friends: to Emina and Nina, who are always the first ones to read my stories, and Ivana, Marina and Anamarija, who celebrate each milestone with me like it's their own.

You really are the best.

I'd also like to thank my wonderful cover artist Antonio Filipović, who masterfully illustrated the cover of this book. I have been fangirling over his comics for quite some time, and it's an honor to have his art grace the cover. To see more of his stunning work, please head over to IG and find him at @a.th.a.n.

And lastly, a warm thank you goes to my parents, who bravely endure a horror-writing daughter without many complaints (and cook her tasty meals as well). Cheers to many more horror stories and lunches.

AUTHOR'S NOTE:

I first heard the phrase "dear heart" (which Lela uses as a term of endearment) in the song "The Horror and the Wild" by The Amazing Devil, and I just couldn't resist putting it in the story. Thank you to The Amazing Devil for writing such beautiful lyrics. Go give them a listen!

ABOUT THE AUTHOR

Ivana Geček is a writer and comic artist currently based in Varaždin, Croatia. She writes satire- and comedy-fueled speculative fiction, with horror and dark fantasy taking up a special place in her heart. Her writing is often set in the hills of her native Zagorje, where she likes to revisit old Slavic creatures, werewolves and demons, and give a fresh spin on their stories.

Some of her work include the short story The Gentleman's Hat, published in the *Slavic Supernatural* anthology, as well as a couple of short stories over at *Morina kutija*. Her comics can be read in OHOHO zine, Strip-Prefiks, Strop, Komikaze, and CBA comics.

In her spare time she likes to read about cryptids, pick at the banjo, and watch good and bad horror movies. Occasionally, she crawls out of her cave and posts on IG at @ivana_gecek.

ABOUT SHTRIGA

Hidden stories in your pocket.
Scifi, fantasy and horror on the go. Publishing your daily dose of speculative fiction since 2020.
Proud recipient of the ESFS Achievement Award for Best Publisher of speculative fiction in Europe, in 2021.
Visit shtriga.com for more information or follow us on Instagram, TikTok and Facebook @shtrigabooks.

Other books by Shtriga inspired by Slavic folklore and mythology:

Slavic Supernatural: An Anthology of Slavic-Inspired Speculative Fiction
edited by: Vesna Kurilić & Antonija Mežnarić

A Town Called River
by Igor Rendić
urban fantasy trilogy

Books by Antonija Mežnarić:
From the Cradle to the Grave, The Lost Treasure Hunters and Other Tales of Folk Terrors, Mistress of Geese, It Eats Us From the Inside & What Do Nightmares Dream of

www.ingramcontent.com/pod-product-compliance
Lightning Source LLC
LaVergne TN
LVHW010600160826
845677LV00013B/3197

* 9 7 8 9 5 3 8 3 6 0 3 2 9 *